WORLD PEACE
AMAZONS

Living in Paradise

S OCIETY

FIELD TRIP DISASTER

Written by **Derek Fridolfs** | Illustrations by **Dave Bardin**

SCHOLASTIC INC.

Thanks to Bob Gale, for making time travel fun!
— Derek

ISBN 978-1-338-27329-8 (TRADE) ISBN 978-1-338-58959-7 (SSE)

10 9 8 7 6 5 4 3 2 1 19 20 21 22 23

PRINTED IN THE U.S.A. 110
FIRST PRINTING 2019

BOOK DESIGN BY CHEUNG TAI
ADDITIONAL ILLUSTRATIONS BY ARTFUL DOODLERS LTD.

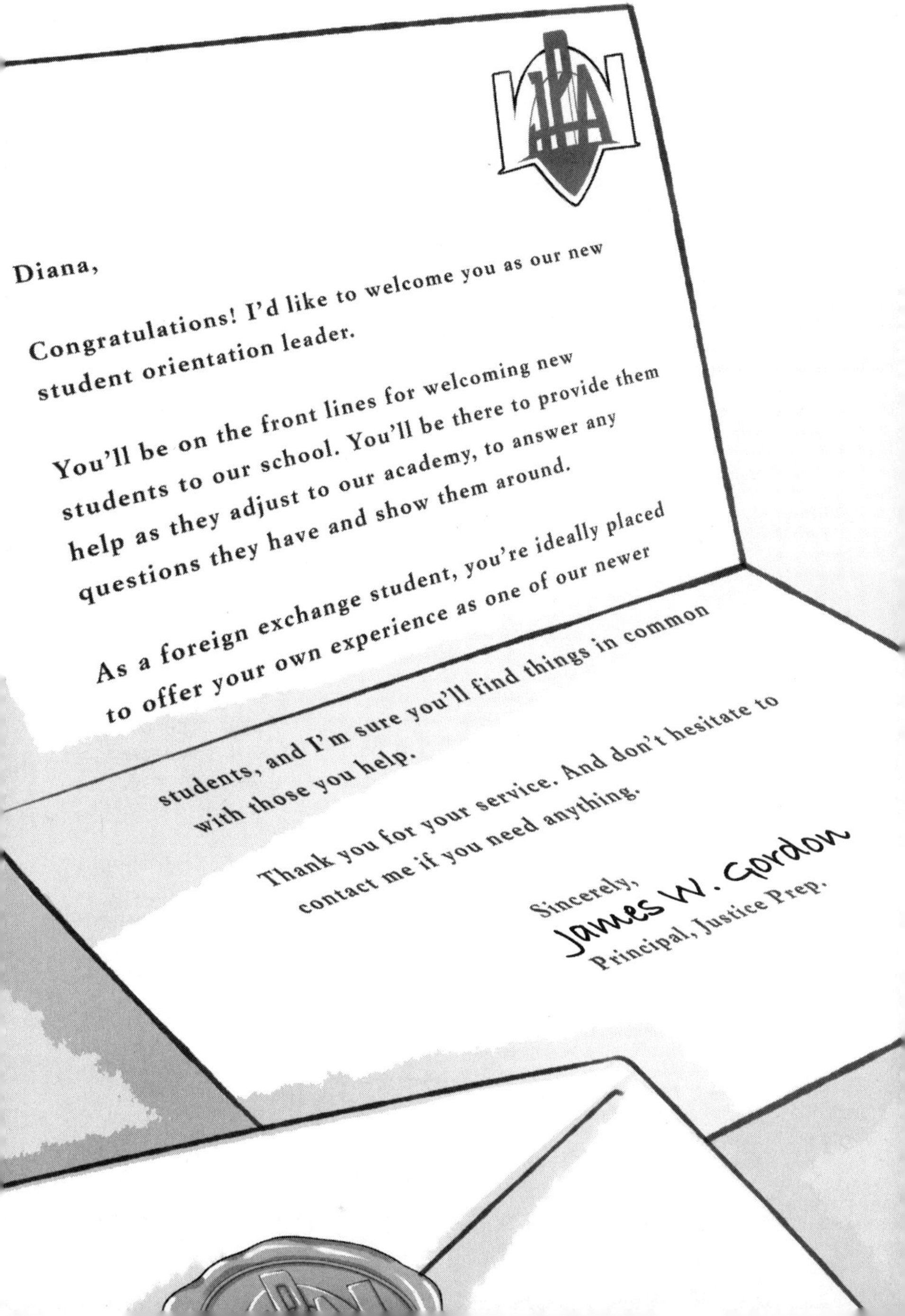

Diana,

Congratulations! I'd like to welcome you as our new student orientation leader.

You'll be on the front lines for welcoming new students to our school. You'll be there to provide them help as they adjust to our academy, to answer any questions they have and show them around.

As a foreign exchange student, you're ideally placed to offer your own experience as one of our newer students, and I'm sure you'll find things in common with those you help.

Thank you for your service. And don't hesitate to contact me if you need anything.

Sincerely,
James W. Gordon
Principal, Justice Prep.

Welcome to Justice Prep!

Here are a few rules to become a great student at our academy:

- Be polite.
- Listen to others.
- Be responsible and prepared.
- Be respectful.
- Be truthful and honest.
- Do your best!
- And always be peaceful.

I'm here to answer all your questions.

And if there's anything I don't know, then we'll go find out together.

HI, DIANA! YOU'RE HERE EARLY.
SOME OF US JUST CAN'T WAIT TO START THE DAY.
UGH. I'D RATHER GO BACK TO BED. IN MY CAVE.
YOU GUYS . . . I'M THE NEW STUDENT ORIENTATION LEADER!!
SO WHO ROPED YOU INTO THIS?
I VOLUNTEERED.
WELL, I THINK IT'S GREAT!

WHAT'S THE MATTER?
THE ASSISTANT THEY ASSIGNED ME ISN'T HERE YET.
I'D HATE TO START WITHOUT PRISCILLA.
PRISCILLA RICH? THE CHEETAH GIRL?! *AND SHE'S RUNNING LATE?!*
THERE'S EVIL AFOOT!
UM, EXCUSE ME. HI THERE. I'M YOUR NEW ORIENTATION ASSISTANT.
ETTA CANDY. PLEASED TO MEET YOU.
I WONDER WHAT HAPPENED TO PRISCILLA?
NOT SURE ABOUT THAT. BUT I'M HERE TO HELP.
THAT SOUNDS GOOD TO ME, ETTA.

REPORT CARD

STUDENT: Etta Candy
LEVEL: Three
HOMEROOM: Gordon
SEMESTER: One

Subject	Grade
READING	A
WRITTEN COMMUNICATION	A
MATHEMATICS	B
SCIENCE/HEALTH	C
SOCIAL STUDIES	B
ART	A
MUSIC	B
PHYSICAL EDUCATION	B

FAVORITE CLASSES: Is lunch a class? I have a sweet tooth. But I also like to read and write.

ATTENDANCE: Great attendance. Never absent. Sometimes tardy.

EXTRA QUALIFICATIONS: I'm told I have unbridled enthusiasm, boldness, school spirit, and a happy attitude. Many have called me "chatty" or "plucky," which is a fun word to say. Many of my teachers report I exceeded their expectations but can be too energetic, as if that's a thing. I look forward to working with you!

NEW STUDENT ORIENTATION FORM

- Take a tour of the school campus, playgrounds, cafeteria, gym, music room, theater, computer labs, and library.
- Explain classroom routines.
- Explain the school dress code.
- Assign lockers.
- Take the students to meet the principal and office staff.

LIST OF NEW STUDENTS

Karen Starr
Ralph Dibny
Caroline Ferris
Imra Ardeen

HOW IS THE TOUR GOING SO FAR? IS THERE ANYTHING ELSE YOU'D LIKE TO GO SEE?
YOU FORGOT THE MOST IMPORTANT THING, DIANA.
WHERE THE VENDING MACHINES ARE!
WOO WOO!! THESE ONES HAVE THE BEST CHOCOLATES IN THEM!
I KNOW THERE'S A LOT TO TAKE IN. BUT YOU'RE ALL SO QUIET.
ANY QUESTIONS? HOW ABOUT YOU IN THE BACK?
WHERE'D SHE GO?
IT'S THE CANDY, DIANA . . . CANDY!

September 3rd

DIANA'S JOURNAL

I'm so thankful to be our school's new orientation leader. I figured it would be a nice chance to establish a good relationship with all the new students, the teachers, and see the school in a new light.

The first day of orientation went well, I think. At first I was worried when Priscilla didn't show up, but they assigned me another assistant in the nick of time.

What can I say about Etta? She's got so much energy and enthusiasm, it almost can't be contained inside of her. I wonder if it's because of all the sugar she eats. But I kinda think that's just who she is. It is a breath of fresh air to have someone excited to hang out with. It's so much different than my other friends. I mean, Clark is nice. And Bruce . . . well, Bruce is Bruce.

Still, I wonder whatever happened with Priscilla. I mean, we never much got along. But I hoped this would be a chance to work together and change that. I hope to have that opportunity again.

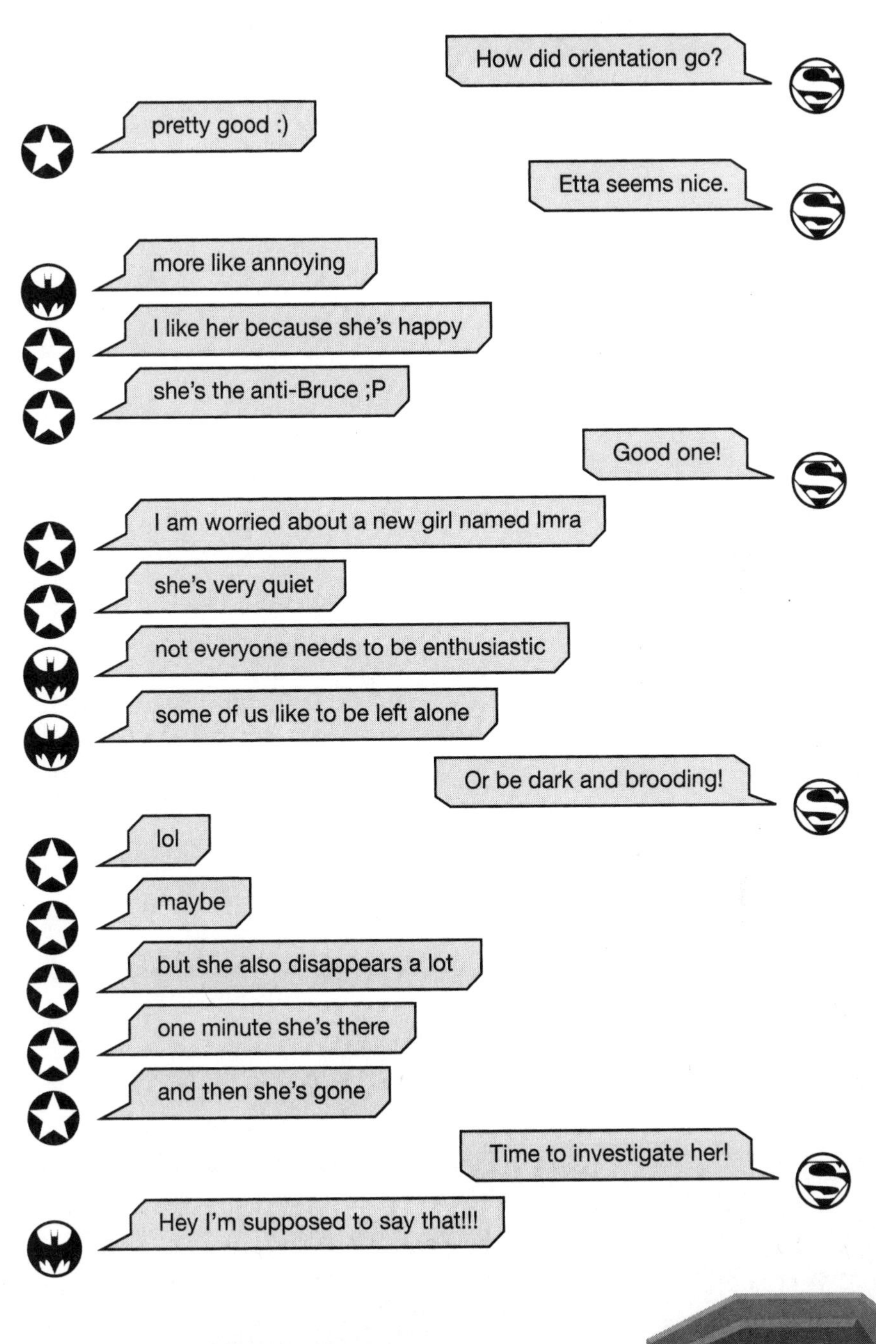
MESSAGES
GROUP CHAT
How did orientation go?
pretty good :)
Etta seems nice.
more like annoying
I like her because she's happy
she's the anti-Bruce ;P
Good one!
I am worried about a new girl named Imra
she's very quiet
not everyone needs to be enthusiastic
some of us like to be left alone
Or be dark and brooding!
lol
maybe
but she also disappears a lot
one minute she's there
and then she's gone
Time to investigate her!
Hey I'm supposed to say that!!!
SEND

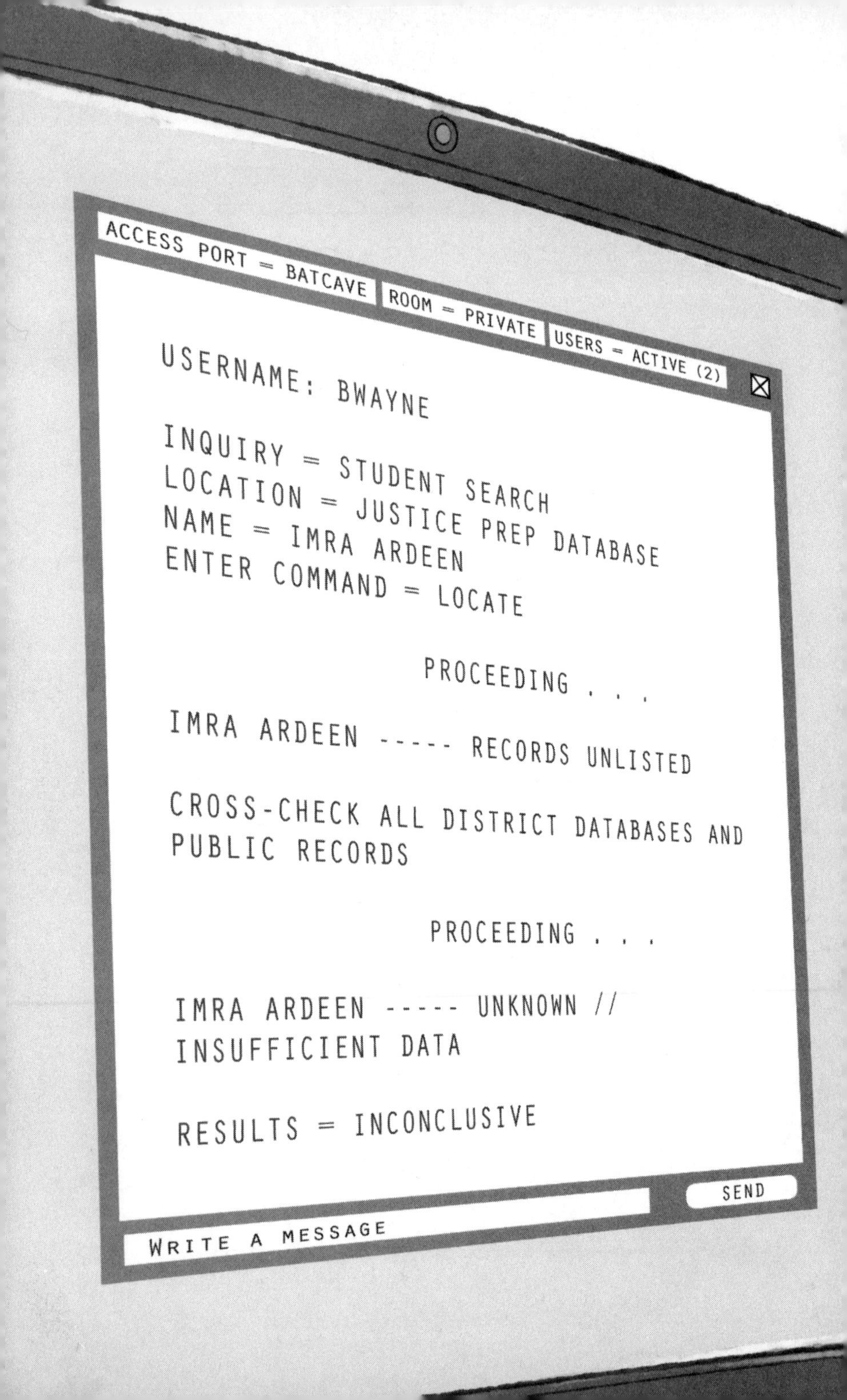

ACCESS PORT = BATCAVE | ROOM = PRIVATE | USERS = ACTIVE (2)

USERNAME: BWAYNE

INQUIRY = STUDENT SEARCH
LOCATION = JUSTICE PREP DATABASE
NAME = IMRA ARDEEN
ENTER COMMAND = LOCATE

PROCEEDING . . .

IMRA ARDEEN ----- RECORDS UNLISTED

CROSS-CHECK ALL DISTRICT DATABASES AND PUBLIC RECORDS

PROCEEDING . . .

IMRA ARDEEN ----- UNKNOWN //
INSUFFICIENT DATA

RESULTS = INCONCLUSIVE

SEND

WRITE A MESSAGE

INTERVIEW RECORD SHEET
FIELD REPORTER – C. KENT

Question 1: Do you know who Imra Ardeen is?

"Whozzat?" – Harleen Quinzel

"I'm afraid not. But I'm fairly new to this school, too." – Arthur Curry

"Isn't she one of the newbies? Big deal." – Doris Zeul

"That's a funny name. Imra be right back with an answer. HAH!" – Joe Kerr

Question 2: Have you talked to Imra?

"Nope nopey nope." – Harleen Quinzel

"I haven't even seen her around, which makes no sense." – Mari McCabe

"She never talks to anyone. That's pretty cold." – Louise Lincoln

"No. Kind of a wallflower." – Pamela Isley

"It's the quiet ones you have to worry about." – Selina Kyle

Question 3: Is there anything you can tell me about Imra? (Where is she from? What school did she transfer from?)

"I think I saw her in the computer lab. Maybe she's a techie!" – Vic Stone

"Hands off, Clark. Don't horn in on my exclusive interview with her." – Lois Lane

"I hear she has a great disappearing act. We should exchange notes." – Zatanna

ANY LUCK FINDING ANYTHING ABOUT IMRA?
OOOH . . . ARE YOU GUYS HAVING A SECRET MEETING?
CAN I BE PART OF YOUR HUSH-HUSH WINK-WINK CLUB?
YOU CAN TEXT ME LATER.
IS IT SOMETHING I SAID? DID I MESS IT UP AGAIN?
YOU KNOW BOYS. BUT HERE, YOU CAN HAVE MY CANDY BAR.
CONSOLATION PRIZE ACHIEVED. WOO!

MESSAGES
GROUP CHAT
is everyone there?
not everyone hopefully
oh don't worry about Etta
she's harmless
what did you find out about Imra?
she doesn't exist
at least not on any school or computer database in any district EVER
and I checked them all
That doesn't make any sense. How is that possible?
she's hiding something and doesn't want to be found
like you in your cave! :)
ugh
I interviewed a lot of students. And no one seems to know her either.
I also checked about Priscilla
you did? where is she?
I borrowed some files from the school office
"borrowed"?
don't worry I put them back
after I got hi-res scans and uploaded them into my computer database
SEND

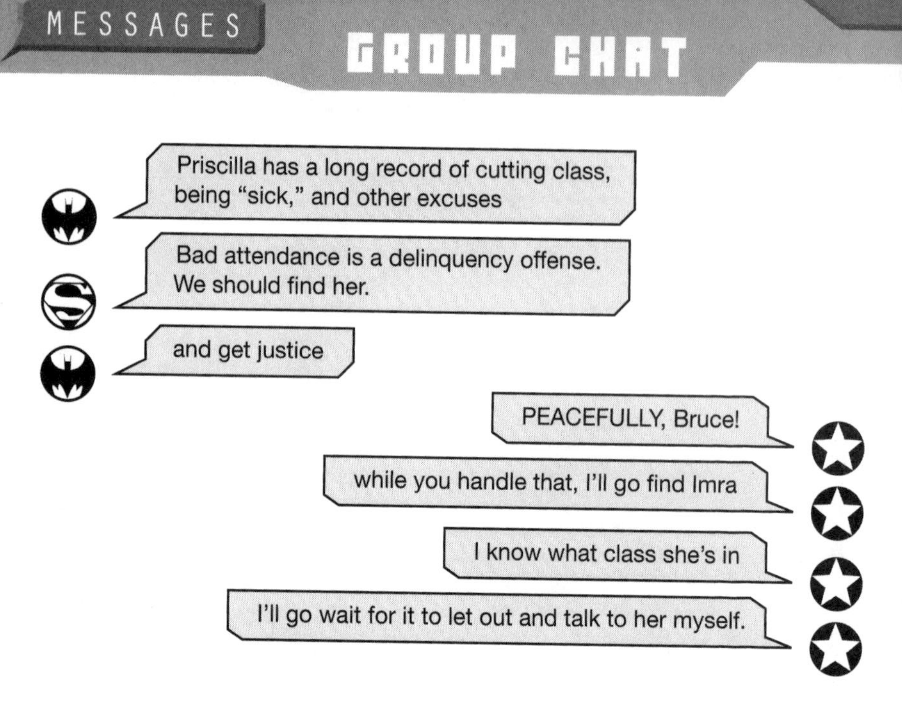
MESSAGES
GROUP CHAT
Priscilla has a long record of cutting class, being "sick," and other excuses
Bad attendance is a delinquency offense. We should find her.
and get justice
PEACEFULLY, Bruce!
while you handle that, I'll go find Imra
I know what class she's in
I'll go wait for it to let out and talk to her myself.
SEND

DIANA, IT'S GOOD I FOUND YOU!
IMRA? I WAS JUST COMING TO FIND YOU
THE SCHOOL OFFICE HAS SOME . . . UH . . . CONCERNS. THEY DON'T HAVE ANY RECORDS ON YOU.
SORRY. TOO TOUGH TO EXPLAIN EVERYTHING HERE. BUT IT'S EXTREMELY IMPORTANT THAT YOU FIND OUT THE TRUTH. AND MAYBE FIX IT.
CLICK
HEY, B— OPEN A DOOR FOR ME TO COME HOME.
I KNEW IT! SHE'S A VILLAIN! GRAB HER!
IMRA? WHAT'S SHE DOING TO DIANA?
DIANA? CLARK? BRUCE? HMM . . . THEY MUST'VE LEFT WITHOUT ME.
I'LL JUST WAIT HERE UNTIL THEY COME BACK. WHAT SHOULD I DO TO PASS THE TIME?

Where are we?
The future
Imra, how is your voice inside my head?
Telepathy
It's a power I have to communicate directly to you
Also you can call me Saturn Girl
It's what everyone calls me here
GET OUT OF MY HEAD!
It's entirely harmless
I'm not reading your mind, only sharing my thoughts with you
Your brain remains safe
NOT YOU, TOO!
heh heh
Let me take you to our base of operations
Our vid-terminal will be able to answer all your questions

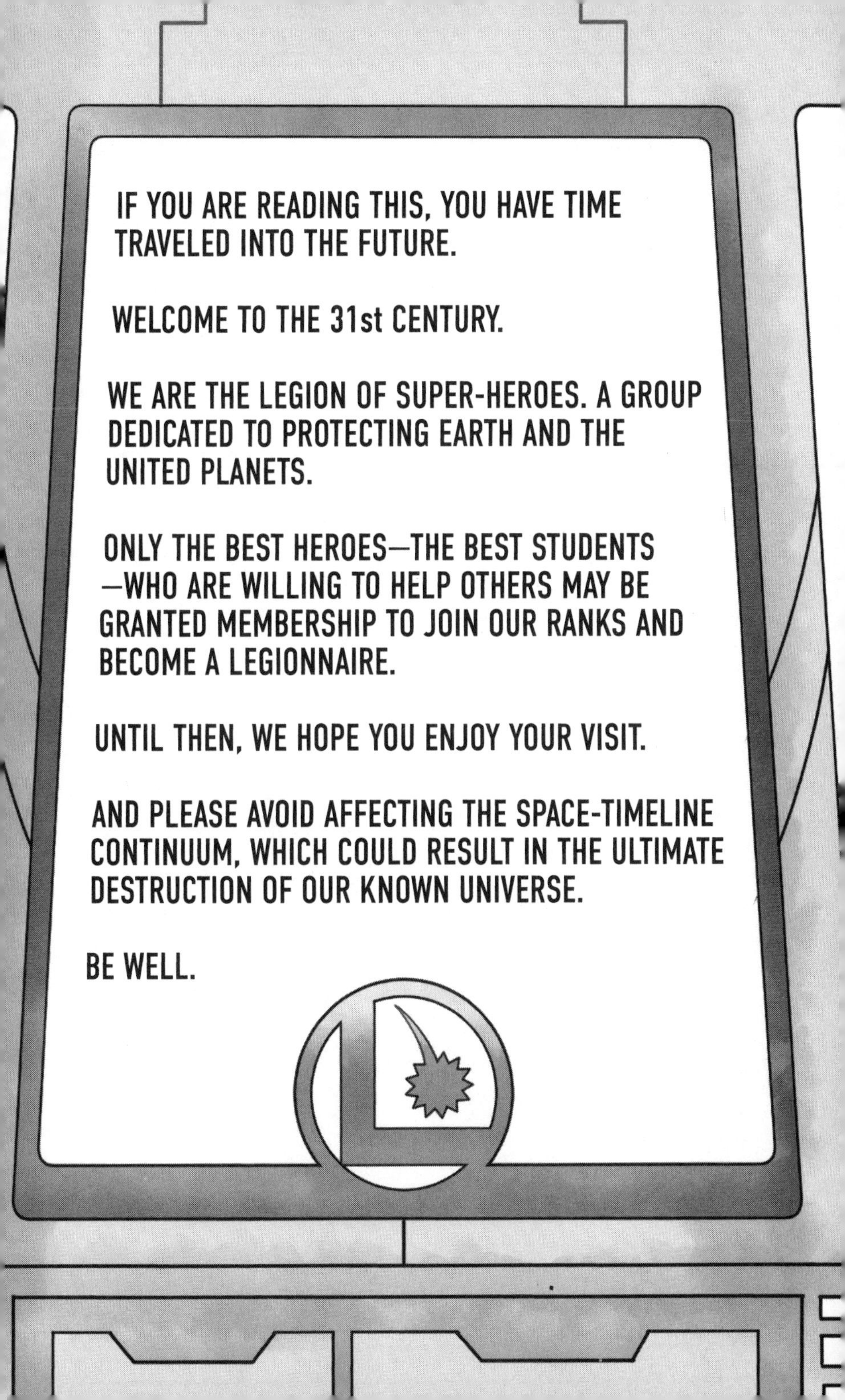

IF YOU ARE READING THIS, YOU HAVE TIME TRAVELED INTO THE FUTURE.

WELCOME TO THE 31st CENTURY.

WE ARE THE LEGION OF SUPER-HEROES. A GROUP DEDICATED TO PROTECTING EARTH AND THE UNITED PLANETS.

ONLY THE BEST HEROES—THE BEST STUDENTS —WHO ARE WILLING TO HELP OTHERS MAY BE GRANTED MEMBERSHIP TO JOIN OUR RANKS AND BECOME A LEGIONNAIRE.

UNTIL THEN, WE HOPE YOU ENJOY YOUR VISIT.

AND PLEASE AVOID AFFECTING THE SPACE-TIMELINE CONTINUUM, WHICH COULD RESULT IN THE ULTIMATE DESTRUCTION OF OUR KNOWN UNIVERSE.

BE WELL.

LEGION OF SUPER-HEROES

LIGHTNING LAD / Garth Ranzz
Founding Member
Powers: Electricity, weather control
"Most Likely to Shock You"

SATURN GIRL / Imra Ardeen
Founding Member
Powers: Telepathy, mind control
"Most Likely to Read Your Mind"

COSMIC BOY / Rokk Krinn
Founding Member
Powers: Magnetism manipulation
"Best Personality"

PHANTOM GIRL / Tinya Wazzo
Powers: Intangibility (can phase through objects)
"Most Likely to Scare You"

BOUNCING BOY / Chuck Taine
Powers: Inflatable body, athletic bouncing
"Most Likely to Drink Your Soda Pop"

TIMBER WOLF / Brin Londo
Powers: Super-human strength, speed, and agility; sharp claws, enhanced senses, rapid healing
Voted "Best Hair" and "Most Likely to Howl at the Moon"

MEMBERSHIP YEARBOOK

CHAMELEON BOY / Reep Daggle
Powers: Shape-shifter
"Best Imitator"

INVISIBLE KID / Lyle Norg
Powers: Undetectable
"Most Likely to Disappear"

COLOSSAL BOY / Gim Allon
Powers: Grow and shrink body; super-human strength and mass
"Biggest Smile"

STAR BOY / Thom Kallor
Powers: Ability to increase an object's mass, density, or gravity
"Most Likely to Become a Star"

TRIPLICATE GIRL / Luornu Durgo
Powers: Ability to divide into three identical bodies
"Triple Threat"

SHRINKING VIOLET / Salu Digby
Powers: Shrink to atomic size
"Tiniest Laugh"

I LIKE YOUR NEW LOOK!
THANKS.
THE REASON I BROUGHT YOU HERE IS OF GRAVE CONCERN.
I NEED YOU TO HELP ME FIX THE TIMELINE.
YOU'RE SOMEHOW INVOLVED IN A PLOT TO DESTROY THE UPCOMING GALACTIC PEACE SUMMIT.
ME?! HOW?!

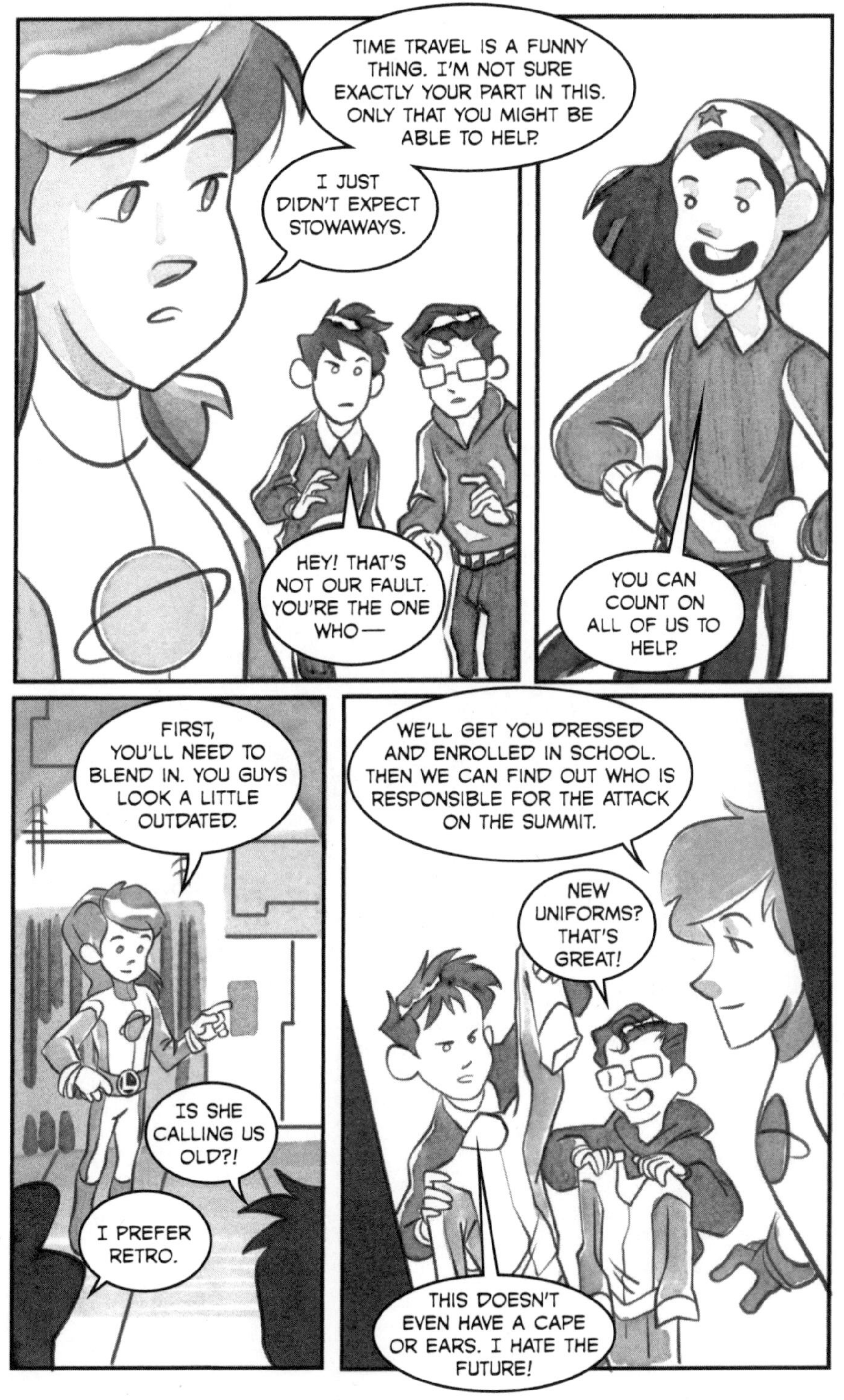
TIME TRAVEL IS A FUNNY THING. I'M NOT SURE EXACTLY YOUR PART IN THIS. ONLY THAT YOU MIGHT BE ABLE TO HELP.
I JUST DIDN'T EXPECT STOWAWAYS.
HEY! THAT'S NOT OUR FAULT. YOU'RE THE ONE WHO—
YOU CAN COUNT ON ALL OF US TO HELP.
FIRST, YOU'LL NEED TO BLEND IN. YOU GUYS LOOK A LITTLE OUTDATED.
IS SHE CALLING US OLD?!
I PREFER RETRO.
WE'LL GET YOU DRESSED AND ENROLLED IN SCHOOL. THEN WE CAN FIND OUT WHO IS RESPONSIBLE FOR THE ATTACK ON THE SUMMIT.
NEW UNIFORMS? THAT'S GREAT!
THIS DOESN'T EVEN HAVE A CAPE OR EARS. I HATE THE FUTURE!

LEGION UNIFORM

Advanced polyfiber suit.
Nanite-linked under-texture provides durable protection from harm and temperature-controlled comfort.

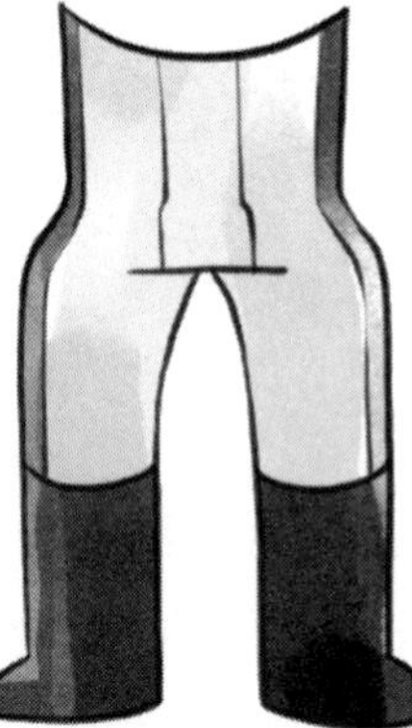

LEGION BELT

Buckle communicator, homing device; with warp-field accessibility.

FLIGHT RING

Composed of the compound Valorium, with antigravity capabilities, allowing the user to fly at super-sonic speed. Willpower activated with near unlimited potential. Flashlight capabilities and can lift objects.

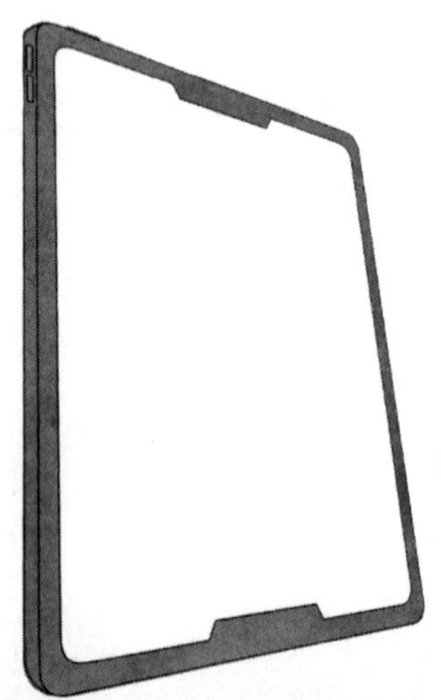

DATA-PAD

Thin, hi-tech, and instantly portable. Who needs a backpack or computer to carry and do your homework?

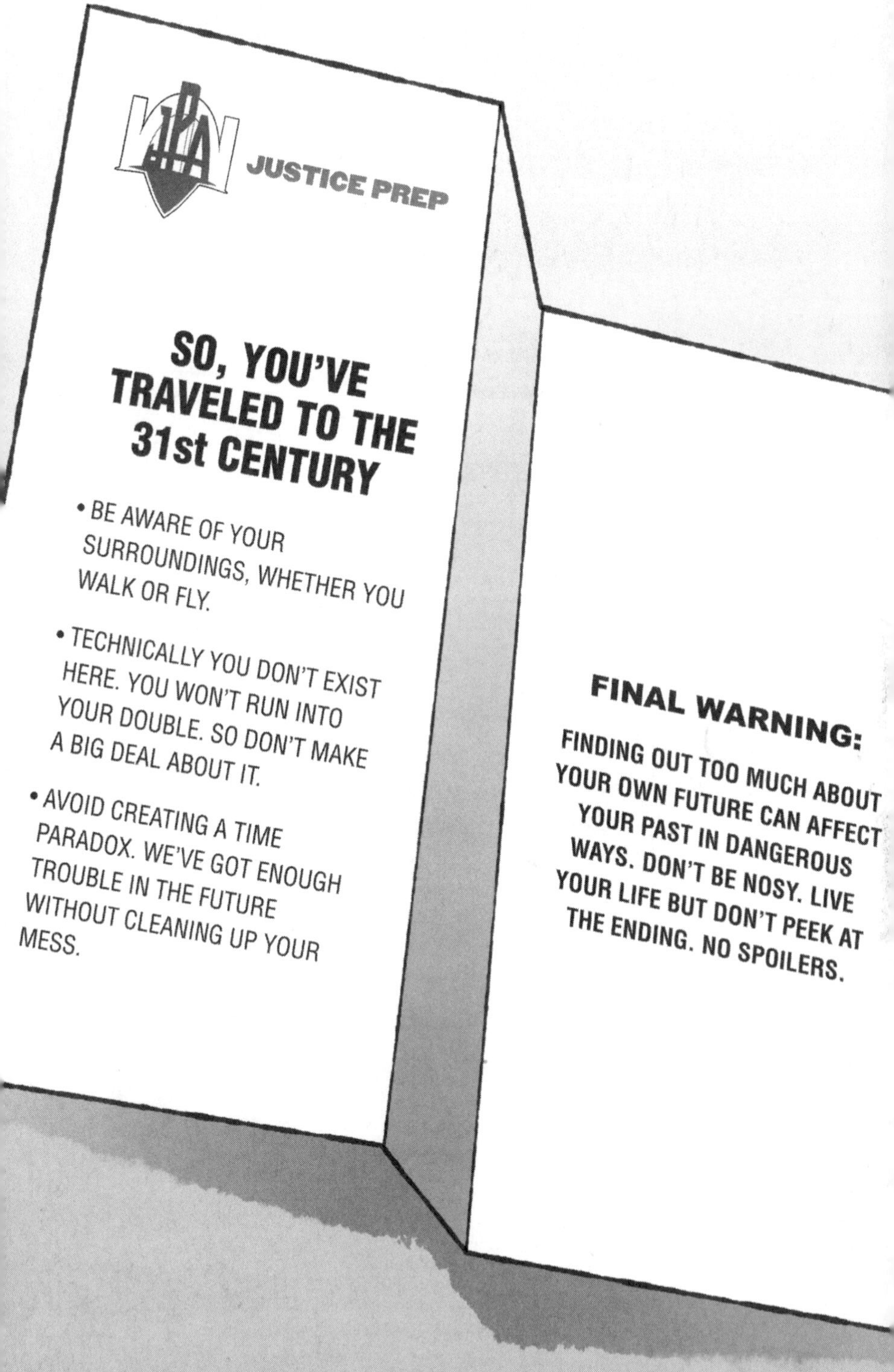

JUSTICE PREP

SO, YOU'VE TRAVELED TO THE 31st CENTURY

- BE AWARE OF YOUR SURROUNDINGS, WHETHER YOU WALK OR FLY.
- TECHNICALLY YOU DON'T EXIST HERE. YOU WON'T RUN INTO YOUR DOUBLE. SO DON'T MAKE A BIG DEAL ABOUT IT.
- AVOID CREATING A TIME PARADOX. WE'VE GOT ENOUGH TROUBLE IN THE FUTURE WITHOUT CLEANING UP YOUR MESS.

FINAL WARNING:

FINDING OUT TOO MUCH ABOUT YOUR OWN FUTURE CAN AFFECT YOUR PAST IN DANGEROUS WAYS. DON'T BE NOSY. LIVE YOUR LIFE BUT DON'T PEEK AT THE ENDING. NO SPOILERS.

HELLO, EVERYONE. I'M THE ONE RESPONSIBLE FOR OPENING THE TIME PORTAL THAT GOT YOU HERE.
I ALSO MAINTAIN OUR STUDENT BASE OF OPERATIONS.
I'M BRAINIAC 5. BUT YOU CAN JUST CALL ME BRAINY.
IT'S BRAINIAC! STOP HIM!!
I THOUGHT WE ALREADY DID?!
HALT! WE DON'T NEED TO USE OUR FISTS EVERY TIME THERE'S A PROBLEM.
LET'S HEAR WHAT HE HAS TO SAY FIRST.

SILLY ME. I SHOULD'VE REALIZED THIS MIGHT HAPPEN.
I'M THE FIFTH VERSION OF BRAINIAC. THE VERSION YOU'VE MET IN YOUR TIME IS MY EVIL ANCESTOR. AND I'M STILL TRYING TO MAKE UP FOR HIS BAD REPUTATION. REST ASSURED THAT I'M NOT HIM.
I CAN VOUCH. BRAINY HERE IS ONE OF OUR LONGEST-SERVING MEMBERS IN GOOD STANDING.
IF YOU HAVE ANY PROBLEMS, JUST PRESS YOUR BELT BUCKLE TO TALK TO ME AND I CAN UPLINK USEFUL INFORMATION DIRECTLY TO YOU.
I'M ONLY HERE TO HELP.
I'M SORRY FOR JUMPING TO CONCLUSIONS.
THAT'S OKAY, I'M A BRAINIAC. IT'S UNDERSTANDABLE.
IF YOU'RE NOT OUR ENEMY, THEN WHO SHOULD WE BE WORRIED ABOUT?

LEGION OF SUPER-HEROES ENEMY DATABASE

[THE FATAL FIVE]

EMERALD EMPRESS

Leader of the Fatal Five, Sarya uses a powerful mystical Emerald Eye of Ekron that floats and obeys her mental commands. It can shoot blasts of energy, allows her to fly, and grants super-strength.

THE PERSUADER

An outlaw who wields an atomic axe that can cut through anything. And he has enhanced strength and endurance as a result of living on a high-gravity planet. He was once recruited by the Legion of Super Heroes to help them, but later turned on them.

THAROK

A small-time crook who injured himself, vaporizing half of his body. He was rebuilt with robotic parts, increasing his intelligence and strength. And his robot mind allows him to control Validus.

MANO

A mutant born with an antimatter touch, allowing him to disintegrate anything he touches with his right hand. He once destroyed his home planet by touching it with the full power of his ability. He's forced to wear a special environmental suit to help him breathe.

VALIDUS

An enormous creature with super-human strength, strong enough to tear an entire planet apart with his bare hands. He can fire energy bolts from his brain. And is resistant to harm.

DATA-PAD JOURNAL ENTRY 01
DIANA PRINCE

THE FUTURE IS STRANGE AND INTERESTING, MUCH LIKE MY JOURNEY FROM PARADISE ISLAND TO SCHOOL. THERE ARE LOTS OF ODD AND NEW EXPERIENCES TO LOOK AT IN WONDER. ESPECIALLY THE ADVANCED TECHNOLOGY. I MEAN, THIS JOURNAL IS MY THOUGHTS THAT HAVE BEEN UPLINKED INTO THE DATA-PAD FROM A NEURAL CONNECTION TO MY BRAIN. I DON'T EVEN HAVE TO TYPE THEM OUT!

BUT WE DON'T HAVE TIME TO ENJOY THIS TRIP, BECAUSE WE HAVE TO STOP A DISASTER FROM HAPPENING. AND THEY THINK I'M PARTIALLY RESPONSIBLE FOR IT! I HAVE NO IDEA HOW THAT COULD BE, SINCE I'VE NEVER BEEN HERE BEFORE. I'VE BARELY EVEN TRAVELED ACROSS THE OCEAN TO GO TO SCHOOL.

THANKFULLY I'VE GOT MY FRIENDS CLARK AND BRUCE ALONG TO HELP OUT. IT WASN'T BY CHOICE, AND BRUCE ALREADY IS HATING HAVING TO ADAPT TO THE 31ST CENTURY. BUT I THINK THE THREE OF US, ALONG WITH THE LEGION OF SUPER HEROES, CAN STOP THE UPCOMING THREAT. AT LEAST, I HOPE SO.

DIGITAL HALL MONITOR FOOTAGE
ALERT
12
9
6

3:21

WHERE ARE THE STUDENT LOCKERS?
THERE AREN'T ANY. THE DATA-PAD IS THE ONLY THING STUDENTS CARRY.
THEN WHAT GETS VANDALIZED? WHERE DO THE BULLIES STUFF THEIR VICTIMS INTO?
IN THE FUTURE, EVERYTHING IS DIGITAL.
HEY, LOSER. WELCOME TO YOUR NEW SCHOOL!!! - FATAL FIVE
OW! IT FEELS LIKE SOMEONE PUNCHED MY BRAIN.
YES. THEY CAN ALSO BULLY PSIONICALLY.

SUPER HERO CLUB

Open auditions at the yellow rocket.
Prepare to face three challenges.
See Legion members for details.

Flying in circles?
Creating harmful smoke trails?
Get your jet pack fixed at **OTTO & AL'S REPAIRS**.
Student discount available!

NOVA EXPRESS TRAVEL

Trips to Mars and the solar system.
Book your summer vacation today!

ICE-CREAM EATING COMPETITION

Nine flavors from nine worlds.
Today in the cafetorium.
See Tenzil Kem to sign up!

FIELD TRIP TO THE INTERPLANETARY ZOO

See the new invisible eagle exhibit.
Deadline for permission slips
is this Wednesday.

HISTORY OF THE 21st CENTURY TO THE 31st CENTURY

PROFESSOR MICHAEL JON CARTER

The greatest hero you've never heard of . . .
teaching the greatest class you've never needed,
until now!

INSTRUCTIONAL GOALS

To provide you with my vast knowledge and time-traveling exploits throughout the centuries. You'll be wowed and amazed by my adventures, heroism, and grandiose personal insight into the man, the myth . . . ME!

At the end of this course, you will be able to learn the history of our universe, all the super hero buddies I call friends, and what it takes to be a hero.

Guest lecturers will include Rip Hunter and Blue Beetle (availability pending).

REQUIRED BACKGROUND

Download and read my authorized and unauthorized biography, *Gold Star: The Life and Times of Booster Gold.* And locate any further news-linked articles and vid-eps based on me.

REQUIRED MATERIALS

To successfully complete this course, you will need to bring the following materials to class: your data-pad, recording device (for photos and vid footage), and metallic autographing pens. Head shot photos provided for signatures (for a nominal fee).

Check out my sweet ride!
The Justice League needed my help to defeat Starro.
I saved the day again!
Meeting with my adoring fans.
I totally saved the president. I rock!
GOLD
GRAND OPENING
Fortune 500 welcomes me as their gold standard.
Premiere to my hit movie sequel.
BOOSTER
GOLD
My wall of fame.

DIANA? IS IT REALLY YOU?!
DO I KNOW YOU?
YOU'RE MY BIGGEST FAN, ER, I MEAN, I'M YOUR BIGGEST FAN!!
DON'T ANY OF YOU RECOGNIZE ME? SUPER DUDE? BAT BOY?
SORRY, I'M AFRAID NOT.
I WOULD NEVER LET ANYONE CALL ME BAT BOY.
HOW'S ABOUT NOW? EHH? EHHHHH?
IS HE ONE OF YOUR ARCHENEMIES?
NOT YET, BUT HE'S GETTING THERE.
SKEETS, I WANT A RECORD OF THIS MEETING. SELFIE!
KLIK
AFFIRMATIVE

THAT'S A KEEPER! I'LL UPLOAD THAT TO MY WALL.
BUT IF YOU'RE JUST KIDS AND DON'T RECOGNIZE ME, THEN MAYBE YOU HAVEN'T MET ME YET.
LUCKY YOU!
NAAAHHH . . . IT'S GOTTA BE TIME-TRAVEL SICKNESS AFFECTING YOUR MINDS.
BECAUSE I'M *TOTALLY* FAMOUS AND WOULD BE RECOGNIZED.
DOES NOT COMPUTE
THAT GUY'S ANNOYING.
I GUESS THE GOOD THING ABOUT THIS FUTURE IS YOU'LL NEVER SEE HIM AGAIN.

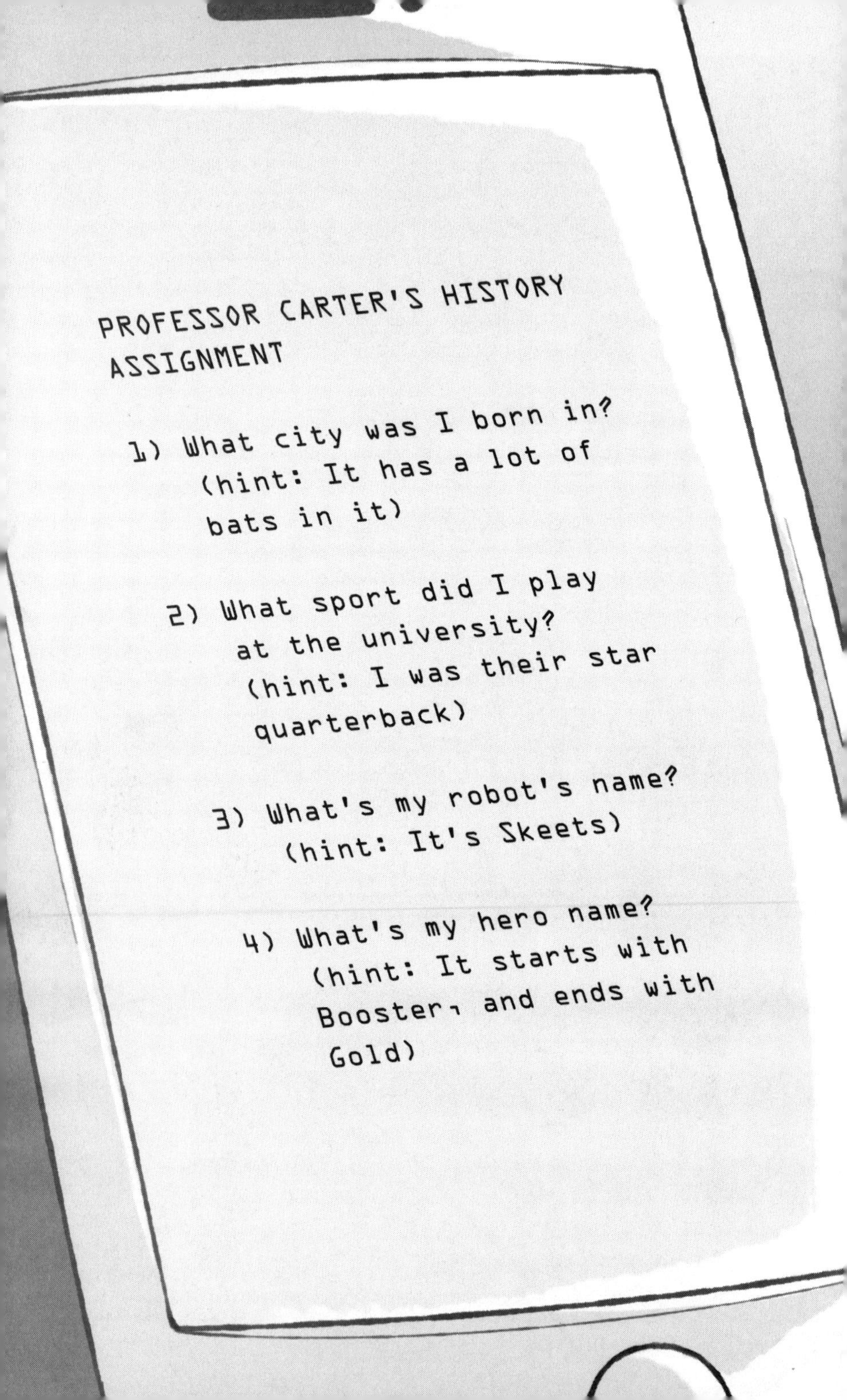

PROFESSOR CARTER'S HISTORY ASSIGNMENT

1) What city was I born in? (hint: It has a lot of bats in it)

2) What sport did I play at the university? (hint: I was their star quarterback)

3) What's my robot's name? (hint: It's Skeets)

4) What's my hero name? (hint: It starts with Booster, and ends with Gold)

Can ya autograph this photo and forward it back?

Also can you autograph some other items in my personal collection?

Like two or three

hundred

Because they'll *TOTALLY* be worth a lot of money someday.

STUDY ALL YOU LIKE
BUT YOU'LL NEVER BE ABLE
TO PASS
THE FATAL FINALS

I'VE BEEN ALERTED THAT THE FATAL FIVE HAVE UPLOADED A COMPUTER VIRUS ONTO YOUR DATA-PADS. I'M CURRENTLY WORKING ON A PATCH TO STOP ANY DAMAGE, AND SHOULD HAVE IT FIXED SHORTLY. SORRY FOR THE TROUBLE.

- BRAINY

How is the timeline affected by me being here?
And how am I responsible for the accident at the peace summit?
All I know is something or someone from your 21st century is responsible
Maybe I'm responsible by traveling into the future
I don't think so
But you might be connected in some way
Whatever happens, we'll stop it
When is the summit?
Tomorrow

Need help with your homework, chores, or work?
Not super-powered enough to do it all yourself?
Get a CLONE today!

Want to learn martial arts?
Learn the tricks of SUPER KARATE!
After-school classes available.
See Val Armorr to sign up.

LOST AND FOUND
Missing arm lost on campus.
If found, please return to Floyd Belkin.
$ $ $ $ $ REWARD $ $ $ $ $

The Legion of Super Heroes doesn't want you—
but we do!
Join the LEGION OF SUBSTITUTE HEROES

Wanna get away from it all?
Manipulate time and space in the comfort of your own alternate world?
Come view the latest in Pocket Universe technology!
Contact the Time Trapper
(not available on weekends).

COME ON. LET'S GO!
BONK
I THINK WE'RE TRYING TO!
DON'T WORRY. I'VE JUST ENROLLED YOU IN A FLIGHT TRAINING COURSE, ALONG WITH ALL YOUR OTHER CLASSES.
BUT KEEP LOOKING FOR ANYONE FROM YOUR CENTURY WHO MIGHT BE HERE TO CAUSE TROUBLE.

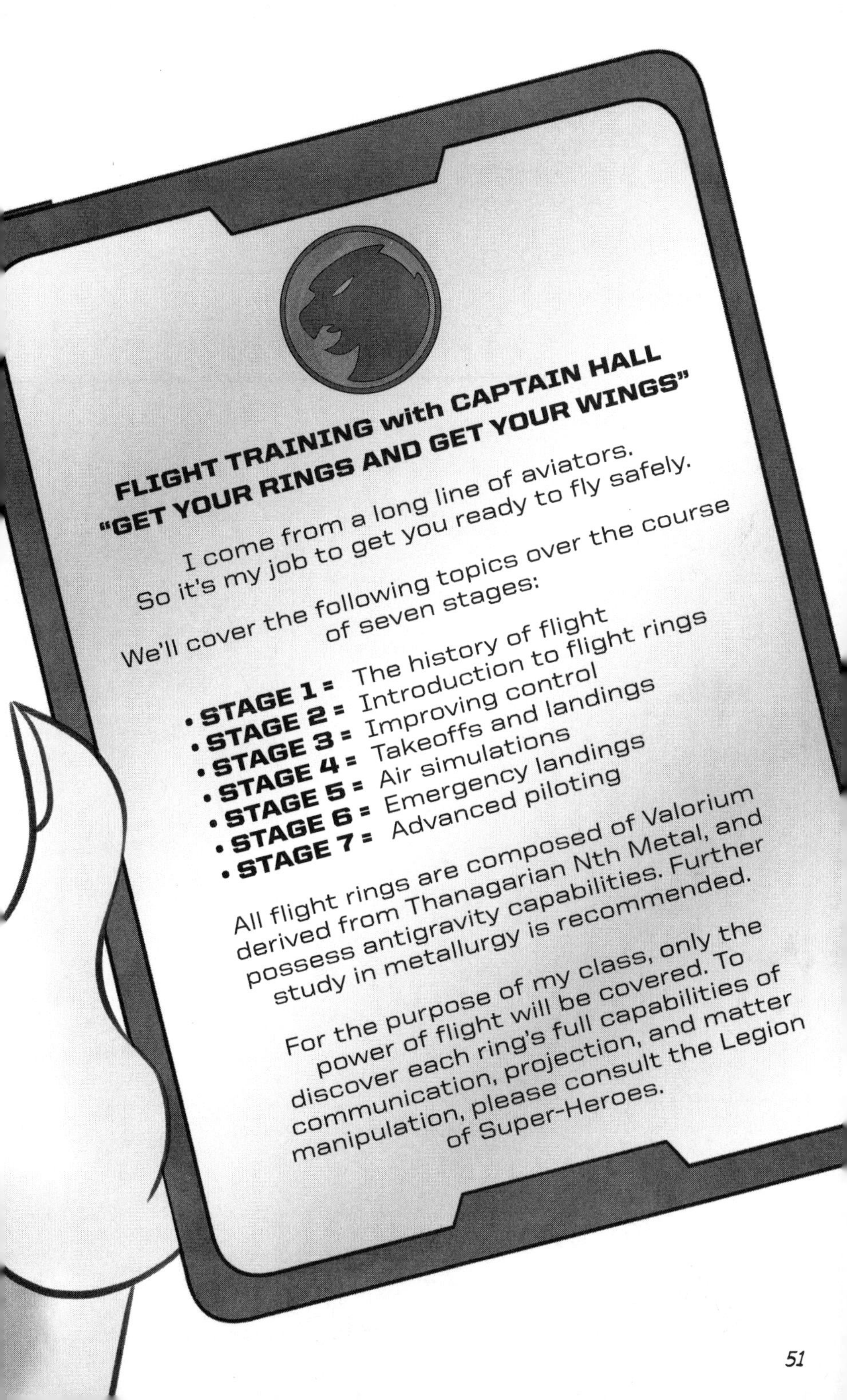
FLIGHT TRAINING with CAPTAIN HALL
"GET YOUR RINGS AND GET YOUR WINGS"
I come from a long line of aviators.
So it's my job to get you ready to fly safely.
We'll cover the following topics over the course of seven stages:
• STAGE 1 = The history of flight
• STAGE 2 = Introduction to flight rings
• STAGE 3 = Improving control
• STAGE 4 = Takeoffs and landings
• STAGE 5 = Air simulations
• STAGE 6 = Emergency landings
• STAGE 7 = Advanced piloting
All flight rings are composed of Valorium derived from Thanagarian Nth Metal, and possess antigravity capabilities. Further study in metallurgy is recommended.
For the purpose of my class, only the power of flight will be covered. To discover each ring's full capabilities of communication, projection, and matter manipulation, please consult the Legion of Super-Heroes.

OKAY. THE POWER OF YOUR FLIGHT RING IS ALL IN YOUR MIND.
IF YOU THINK IT, YOU CAN ACHIEVE IT.
LIKE THIS?
ACTUALLY, I DON'T THINK I NEED THAT RING AFTER ALL. FLIGHT IS ONE OF MY POWERS.
AND WE ALL KNOW THAT YOU CAN DO THIS, RIGHT?
I HAVEN'T ACTUALLY MASTERED IT YET.
HERE GOES NOTHING . . .

AAAAAAAAAAAAAAAA!
GOTCHA, CLARK.
THANKS, DIANA!
NEXT IS BRUCE WAYNE.
NOT FOR ME. I'LL TRANSFER TO DRIVER'S ED.

Burst Your Time Bubble?
Unable to travel where you want?
Vehicular and Time Displacement repair qualified.
Visit the SHOOTER AUTO SHOP.
Call for an evaluation (ask for Jimmy).
TICKETS AVAILABLE
"Around the world in eighty minutes!"
Book passage on the Earth Satellite Tour.
Departing daily from the Jules Verne Observatory.
TUTORING AVAILABLE NOW
Need help finishing your homework or passing your finals?
I have a 99.999999% success rate.
References available.
Msg me @BRAINIAC5
VISIT SOUTH POLE CITY
And the world-famous giant atomic cosmic lamp!
LORI'S PET SHOP
For all your personal pet care or science experiment needs.
The exclusive carrier of colonized Antarian Protean shape-shifters.
Open Monday through Friday.

FUTURE FINANCE

BUSINESS 101

Instructor: Dr. Alexia Luthor
Office Hours: By appointment

How to succeed at business and make a fortune in the 31st century

COURSE DESCRIPTION:

This course emphasizes the demonstration of business and finance strategies using the integration of current methodologies and practices, and skills learned and passed down by many generations of Luthors. By the end of our course, you will have the know-how to make as much money as you can and buy anything you want.

OBJECTIVES:

As a result of this course, you will be able to:

- Identify, locate, and navigate through the business industry
- Explain the theories to the success of LexCorp
- Collaborate effectively with your fellow students to create a framework for business growth and financial success
- Plan strategies to grow your market share
- Describe several effective tools for incorporating, wealth growth, and avoiding hostile takeovers

REQUIRED TEXTS:

- *The World According to Luthor*
- *Lexplinations: How to Become Rich and Powerful*

BUSINESS 101 – HOMEWORK ASSIGNMENT

All businesses require a development plan to establish a new venture as an entrepreneur. Every new venture should be required to come up with a detailed proposal plan. By coming up with a plan in advance, it helps to offset the costs and to budget. A good plan helps establish the vision needed to create a good business. With a plan in place, it helps management to think about the business, the objectives to its workers, and decisions to smooth the progress of planning.

First you need to break up into class groups of four. Decide who will be the boss of the company and who will be the workers. Decide what type of business you want to create and if there's a need for it. And then develop a plan for how to create it.

As a Luthor, my family controlled businesses in many markets, from property to industry to military and financial. Find something that you like, and create a business for it.

CLARK —

COME SEE ME
AFTER CLASS!

DR. ALEXIA

I'M SURE YOU'RE AWARE, THERE'S A LONG HISTORY BETWEEN THE LUTHORS AND YOU.
IT'S NOT ONE I'M PROUD OF.
I UNDERSTAND. BUT I'M LEARNING TO JUDGE THE INDIVIDUAL AND NOT THE FAMILY.
AS FAR AS I'M CONCERNED, YOU SEEM LIKE A GOOD TEACHER.
BUT IF YOU'RE NOT, THEN I'LL BE THE ONE TO SEND YOU TO DETENTION.
JUST ASK YOUR ANCESTOR, LEX.

INTRODUCTION TO DRIVER'S EDUCATION

Instructor: Space Cabbie

You're here because you failed flight training or you just want to learn how to drive a vehicle. And I'm here to teach you. It's up to me to help you identify the basic elements of becoming a successful driver, with the rules and regulations of the road and sky. I've got a lotta miles and experience as a laborer and pilot for hire. And a member of the "Cosmic Order of Space Cab Pilots" and "Veterans of Alien Wars." I also have my teaching credentials.

With that outta the way, here's our objectives:

1) To explain the structure of this here driving program and your responsibility for successful completion.

2) To list the basic driving fundamentals.

3) To identify the impact of decision-making on driving records.

4) To define the laws and restrictions of driving.

5) And to complete the course by obtaining a license.

Fill out and turn in your permission slip to be in this class. Once it's authorized, then go get your keys, meet me in the garage, and let's hit the road or airways. It's time to drive!

I MANAGED TO CREATE AN OFFICIAL PERMISSION SLIP FOR YOUR ENROLLMENT INTO THE CLASS. JUST TURN THIS IN AND YOU SHOULD BE OKAY. DELETE THIS MESSAGE!

– BRAINY

DRIVER'S EDUCATION
CERTIFICATE OF PERMISSION

Name: Bruce Wayne

Learner's Permit Number: 19992001

School/Office Code: 247247247

Parent or guardian's signature: ______________

Teacher's signature: ______________

OKAY, JUST AS YOU LEARNED.
LET'S TAKE OFF NICE AND—
VROOOOOOOM
—EASY!!!
LOOK OUT!
USE YOUR SIGNAL!!
BRAKES . . . BRAKES!!!
KRASHH

MAYBE IT'S SAFER **FOR THE REST OF US . . .** IF SOMEONE JUST DRIVES YOU EVERYWHERE.
HMPFF! EVEN A THOUSAND YEARS IN THE FUTURE, I STILL NEED ALFRED.

AUTO SHOP CLASS

Taught by **THE MAIN MAN**, aka **LOBO**

Office Hours: No

(Special thanks to my friends at the intergalactic police work release program)

Looks like yer in trouble fer wrecking yer car, just like I'm in trouble fer blowing up a planet. As part of our punishment, we're stuck together. So I guess I'll train you how to fix an' upgrade yer vehicle, to get it in tip-top shape to hit the sky.

Hope ya brought some hooks, chains, laser saws, an' power drills. We'll hammer that metal hunka junk you call a car into place. An' once it's fixed, ya owe me a ride. I wanna go see the space dolphins, an' yer my ticket outta here!

WHOA! YOU CRASH THAT AN' WALK AWAY? GOOD ONE, MY MAN!

WHATCHA WAITIN' FER? PICK UP SOME A THOSE DANGEROUS POWER TOOLS AN' LET'S CHOP 'ER UP.

WHAT SHOULD I DO?
HOW SHOULD I KNOW?

SMASH
71490
71490
WHAT HAPPENED TO YOU?
I FOUND MY NEW FAVORITE STUDENT!
71490

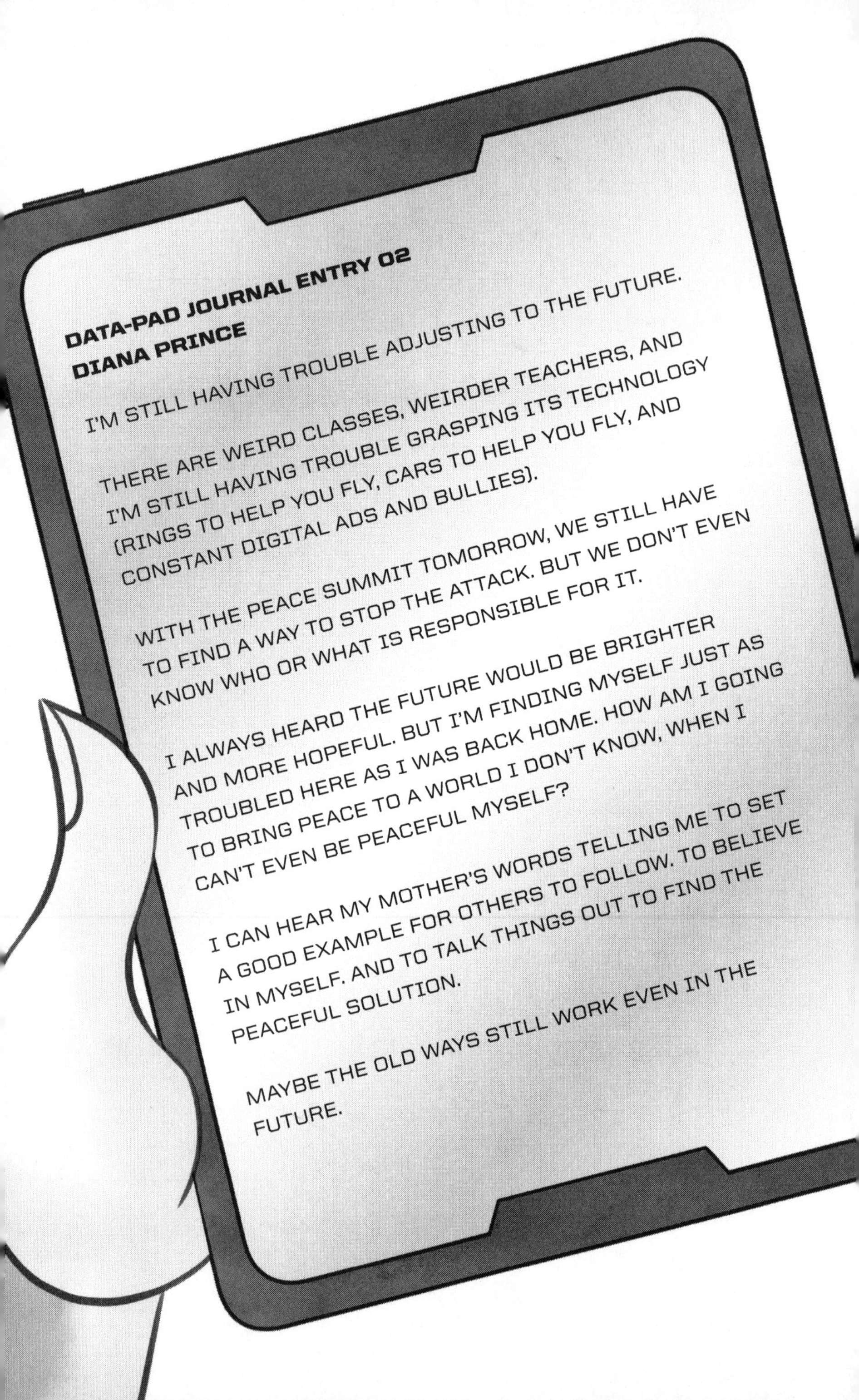

DATA-PAD JOURNAL ENTRY 02
DIANA PRINCE

I'M STILL HAVING TROUBLE ADJUSTING TO THE FUTURE.

THERE ARE WEIRD CLASSES, WEIRDER TEACHERS, AND I'M STILL HAVING TROUBLE GRASPING ITS TECHNOLOGY (RINGS TO HELP YOU FLY, CARS TO HELP YOU FLY, AND CONSTANT DIGITAL ADS AND BULLIES).

WITH THE PEACE SUMMIT TOMORROW, WE STILL HAVE TO FIND A WAY TO STOP THE ATTACK. BUT WE DON'T EVEN KNOW WHO OR WHAT IS RESPONSIBLE FOR IT.

I ALWAYS HEARD THE FUTURE WOULD BE BRIGHTER AND MORE HOPEFUL. BUT I'M FINDING MYSELF JUST AS TROUBLED HERE AS I WAS BACK HOME. HOW AM I GOING TO BRING PEACE TO A WORLD I DON'T KNOW, WHEN I CAN'T EVEN BE PEACEFUL MYSELF?

I CAN HEAR MY MOTHER'S WORDS TELLING ME TO SET A GOOD EXAMPLE FOR OTHERS TO FOLLOW. TO BELIEVE IN MYSELF. AND TO TALK THINGS OUT TO FIND THE PEACEFUL SOLUTION.

MAYBE THE OLD WAYS STILL WORK EVEN IN THE FUTURE.

LUNCH MENU

All of our meals are prepared in our science labs with balanced protein, fiber, and vitamin supplements. Low in fat, low in sugar, and any allergens are removed and adjusted per student requirement. Eat with your friends in the cafetorium, or take it to go with a glass of high-energy natural water.

Today's selection includes:

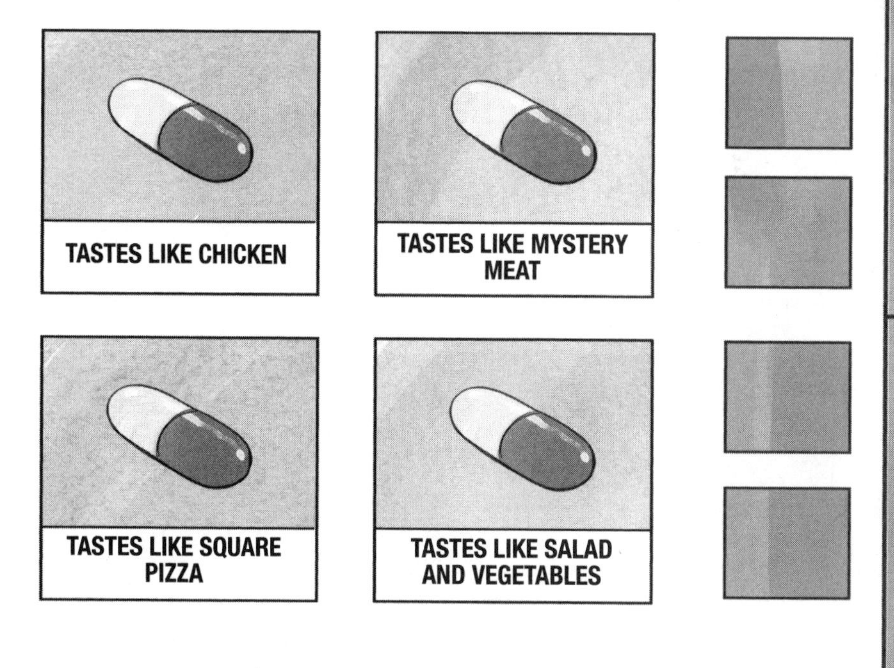

LUNCH SPECIAL

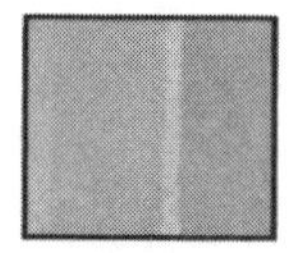

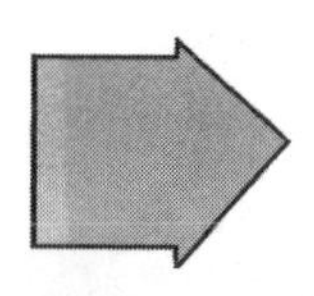

GIMME YOUR LUNCH PILL!
BUT I ALREADY SWALLOWED IT.
BARF IT UP!
LEAVE HIM ALONE.
NOT NOW!!
THAT WAS AWFULLY BIG OF HER TO HELP OUT.
NOW IT'S MY TURN TO DO SOMETHING BIG.

BOINNNG
100 DIGITAL DEMERITS EACH.
FLOAT WITH ME TO THE DETENTION ZONE.
THANKS FOR HELPING OUT! I'M BOUNCING BOY.
AND I'M DIANA.

GIVE
PEACE
A
CHANCE

Have you been able to find anyone from your century yet?
No
I haven't seen anyone I recognize
Is there a library where we can look up more information?
The Hall of Records
Your rings can take you there
I'll walk
I'll carry you
Please don't
Carrying is faster
Diana and I will go compete in the Galaxy Games
We might be able to find who we're looking for there

WOW! THERE'S A LOT OF DIGITAL FILES HERE.
WE SHOULD BE ABLE TO FIND OUT MORE ABOUT THE GALACTIC PEACE SUMMIT. BUT I'M HAVING TROUBLE FINDING ANY INFORMATION ABOUT IT.
I AM C.O.M.P.U.T.O.
A CYBER-CEREBRAL OVERLAPPING MULTIPROCESSOR TRANSCEIVER-OPERATOR.
HOW MAY I ASSIST YOU?
CAN YOU HELP US FIND OUT EVERYTHING ABOUT THE GALACTIC PEACE SUMMIT?
WHAT IS YOUR NAME?
MY NAME IS CLARK KENT, AND THIS IS BRUCE WAYNE.

I AM COMPUTO THE CONQUEROR
YOU ARE MY ENEMY
BRAINY . . . A LITTLE HELP, PLEASE . . .
AN ELECTRICAL FEEDBACK SHOULD SHUT IT DOWN.
I APOLOGIZE. I ORIGINALLY CREATED COMPUTO TO BE GOOD.
I'M BEGINNING TO THINK . . . ALL LIBRARY COMPUTERS ARE EVIL.

THE RULES OF JOUNCE

The goal of the game is to be the last one standing who hasn't been hit by the ball.

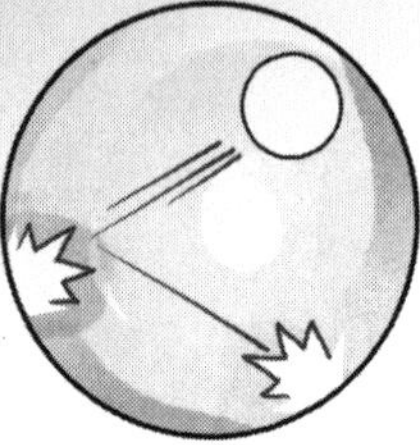

There is no set number of players. The game is played in an enclosed cylindrical antigravity room. As the laser ball enters the room, each time it bounces off the wall, it picks up speed. If your body is hit, you're electrocuted and disqualified. If you catch the laser ball, you have the ability to throw it away or at another player.

There are three rounds. Each period, the ball will increase speed and number:

Round 1 = 1 ball
Round 2 = 2 balls
Round 3 = 3 balls

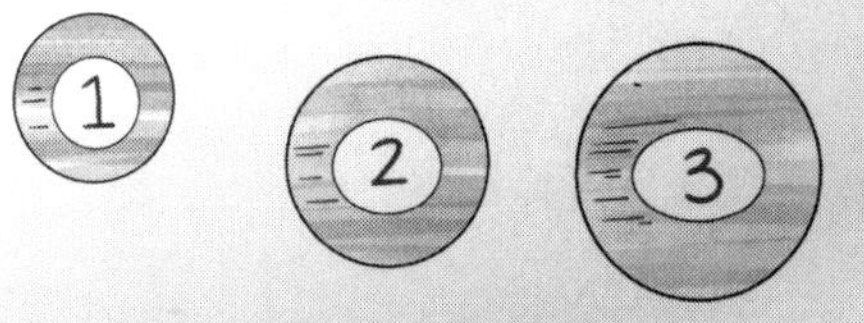

If there is no winner at the end of the third round, then it goes into overtime, where the ball will multiply with each bounce (causing multiple balls to be in play).

PLAYERS' STATS

(Scale of 1–10)

	AGILITY	SPEED	STRENGTH
DIANA PRINCE	8	8	8
SATURN GIRL	9	6	5
LIGHTNING LAD	6	8	6
PHANTOM GIRL	10	5	5
COSMIC BOY	7	5	7
BOUNCING BOY	3	2	10
TRIPLICATE GIRL	8	8	4
VALIDUS	6	6	11
THAROK	6	8	7
MANO	4	3	5

ROUND ONE – BEGIN
ROUND TWO
ROUND THREE

OVERTIME
WINNER – DIANA PRINCE
WHOOOOOSH
POW!
POW!
DIANA HAS BEEN ELIMINATED! BUT WHO THREW THOSE?!
POW!

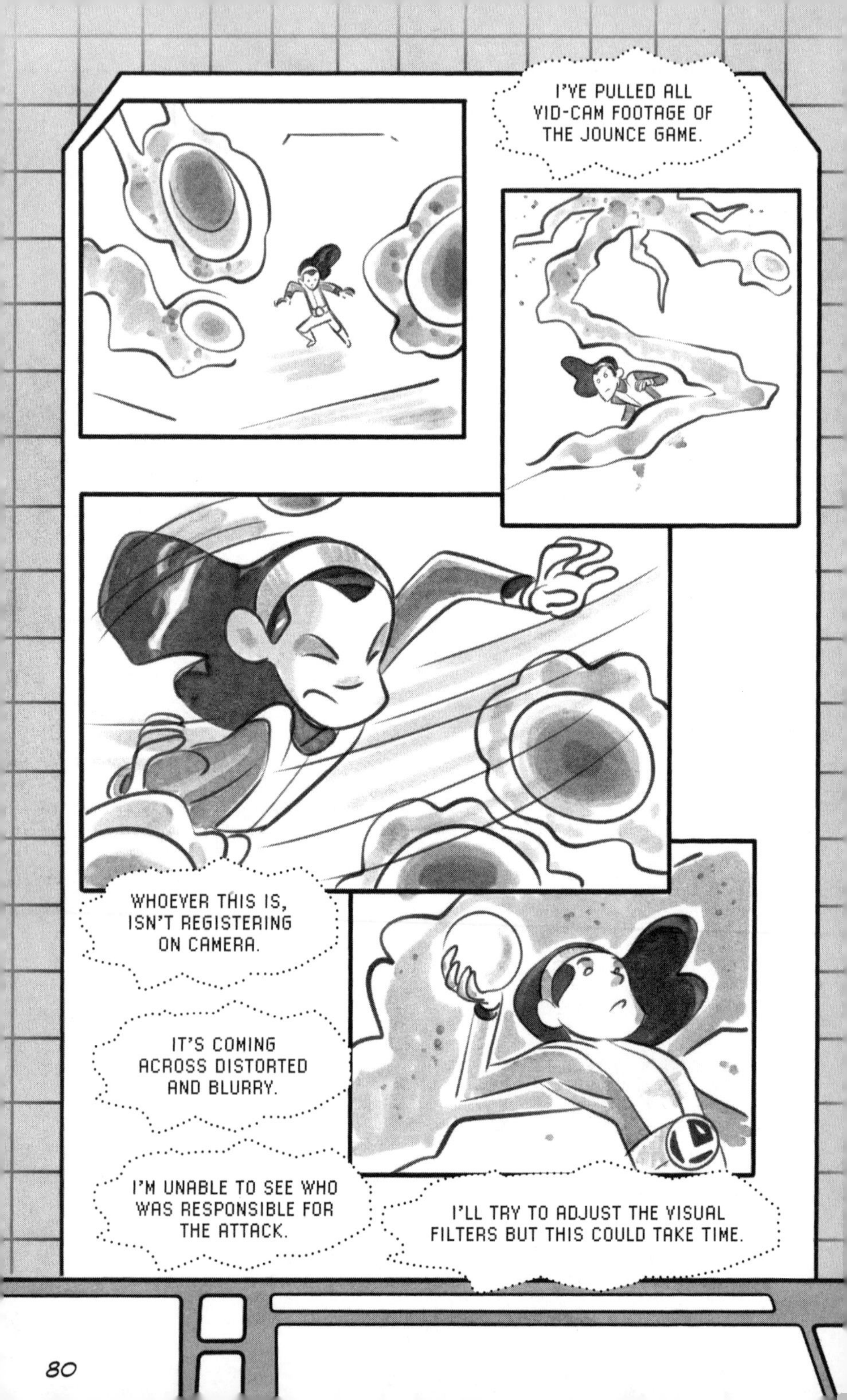
I'VE PULLED ALL VID-CAM FOOTAGE OF THE JOUNCE GAME.
WHOEVER THIS IS, ISN'T REGISTERING ON CAMERA.
IT'S COMING ACROSS DISTORTED AND BLURRY.
I'M UNABLE TO SEE WHO WAS RESPONSIBLE FOR THE ATTACK.
I'LL TRY TO ADJUST THE VISUAL FILTERS BUT THIS COULD TAKE TIME.

I've got my
EYE
on you

I can't believe I lost that game
It wasn't your fault
Someone cheated
Does it have anything to do with that EYE message?
It's possible
The Emerald Eye of Ekron is controlled by the Emerald Empress
She's the leader of the Fatal Five and always a problem
I'm only making things worse by being here in the future
I don't know what I'm doing, I'm a distraction, and I'm lost
Don't worry, being a new student isn't easy
But I'm here to help
That's what I'm supposed to be telling you as the orientation leader
Normally it's against the rules to show you too much
But I'd like you to see something

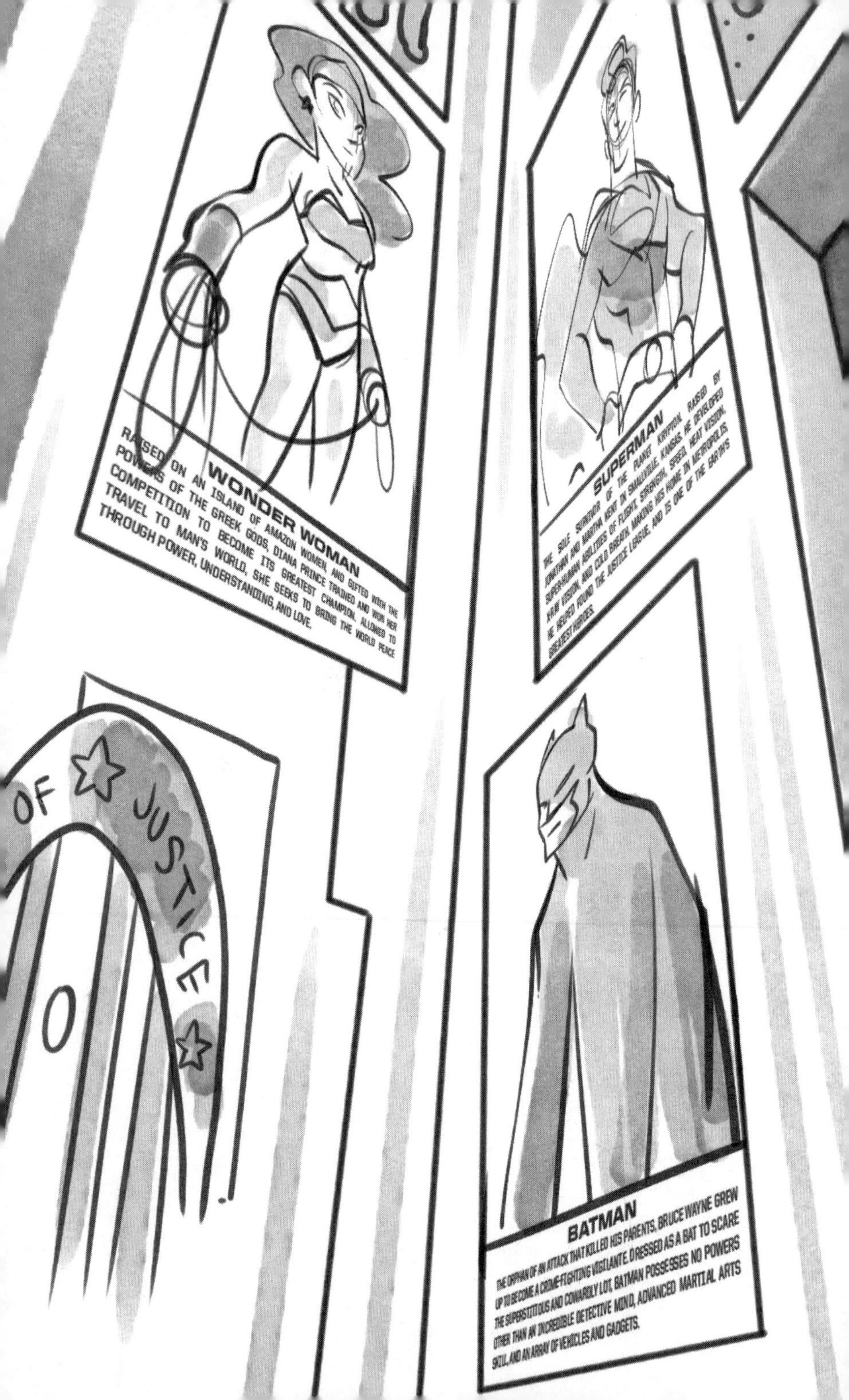
WONDER WOMAN
RAISED ON AN ISLAND OF AMAZON WOMEN, AND GIFTED WITH THE POWERS OF THE GREEK GODS, DIANA PRINCE TRAINED AND WON HER COMPETITION TO BECOME ITS GREATEST CHAMPION. ALLOWED TO TRAVEL TO MAN'S WORLD, SHE SEEKS TO BRING THE WORLD PEACE THROUGH POWER, UNDERSTANDING, AND LOVE.
SUPERMAN
THE SOLE SURVIVOR OF THE PLANET KRYPTON. RAISED BY JONATHAN AND MARTHA KENT IN SMALLVILLE, KANSAS, HE DEVELOPED SUPER-HUMAN ABILITIES OF FLIGHT, STRENGTH, SPEED, HEAT VISION, X-RAY VISION, AND COLD BREATH. MAKING HIS HOME IN METROPOLIS, HE HELPED FOUND THE JUSTICE LEAGUE, AND IS ONE OF THE EARTH'S GREATEST HEROES.
OF JUSTICE
BATMAN
THE ORPHAN OF AN ATTACK THAT KILLED HIS PARENTS, BRUCE WAYNE GREW UP TO BECOME A CRIME-FIGHTING VIGILANTE. DRESSED AS A BAT TO SCARE THE SUPERSTITIOUS AND COWARDLY LOT, BATMAN POSSESSES NO POWERS OTHER THAN AN INCREDIBLE DETECTIVE MIND, ADVANCED MARTIAL ARTS SKILL, AND AN ARRAY OF VEHICLES AND GADGETS.

IS THAT . . . ME?
THAT'S A LOT TO LIVE UP TO.
YOU'RE WRONG. IT'S THE OTHER WAY AROUND.
THAT WOMAN HAS A LOT TO LIVE UP TO, TO BECOME THE HERO THAT YOU ALREADY ARE.

HEY, DIANA. WE DEFEATED ANOTHER EVIL LIBRARY COMPUTER.
WHAT IS THIS PLACE?
THE HALL OF HEROES CELEBRATES YOUR PAST ACCOMPLISHMENTS, AND OTHER HEROES LIKE YOU.
BUT YOU REALLY SHOULDN'T SEE TOO MUCH. IT'S NOT GOOD TO KNOW TOO MUCH ABOUT YOUR OWN FUTURE.
"THE DIANA PRINCE PEACEKEEPERS GARDEN". AND I HAVE AN EXHIBIT NAMED AFTER ME IN THE MUSEUM OF SPACE. WHAT DOES BRUCE HAVE?
I'M SURE THERE'S A SECRET CAVE SOMEWHERE.
WHOOOOOSH

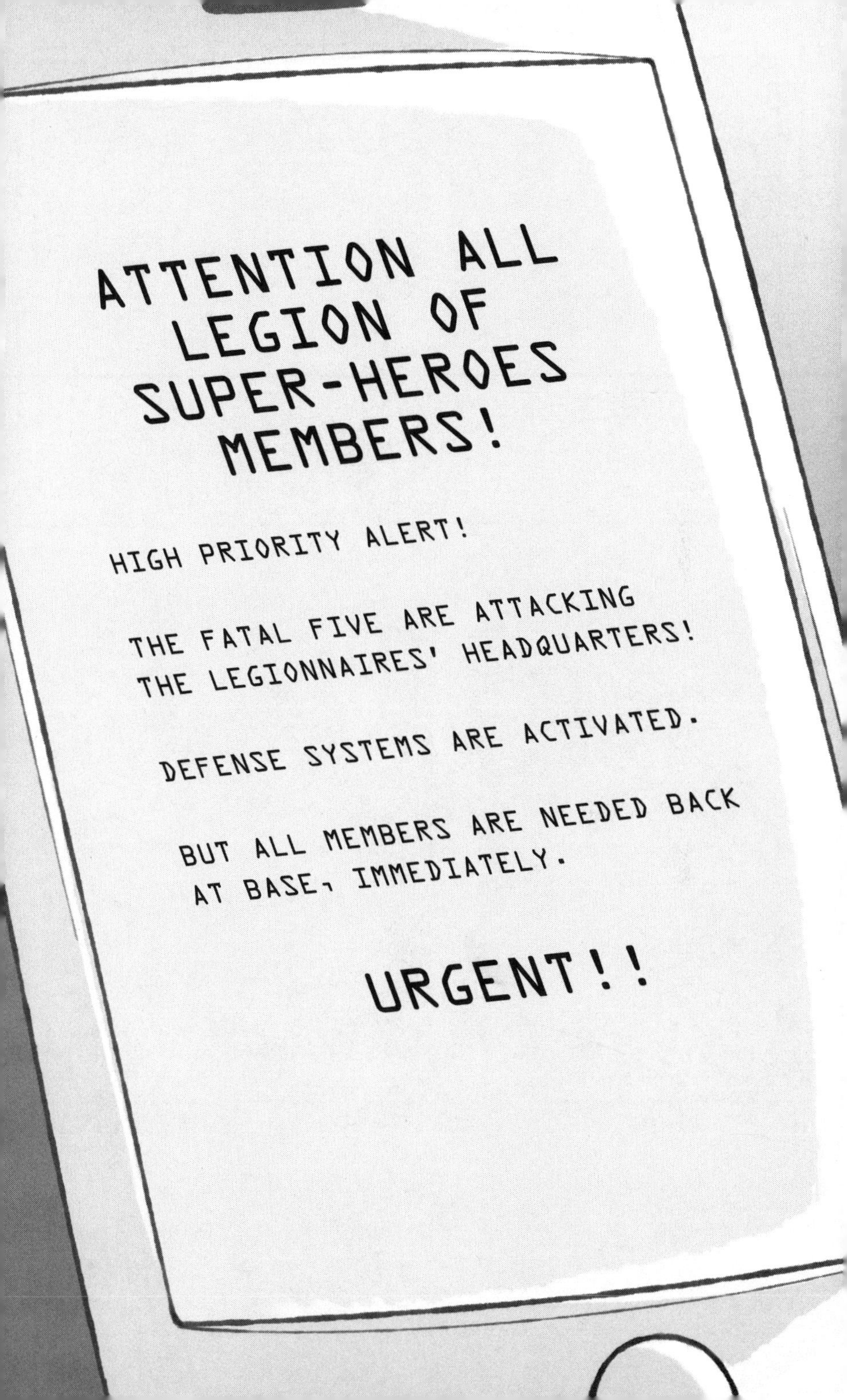

ATTENTION ALL
LEGION OF
SUPER-HEROES
MEMBERS!

HIGH PRIORITY ALERT!

THE FATAL FIVE ARE ATTACKING
THE LEGIONNAIRES' HEADQUARTERS!

DEFENSE SYSTEMS ARE ACTIVATED.

BUT ALL MEMBERS ARE NEEDED BACK
AT BASE, IMMEDIATELY.

URGENT!!

HERE THEY COME!
POW!
FUMP

ANOTHER ALERT?
From the Television Trouble-Finder!
ALEXIA LUTHOR!

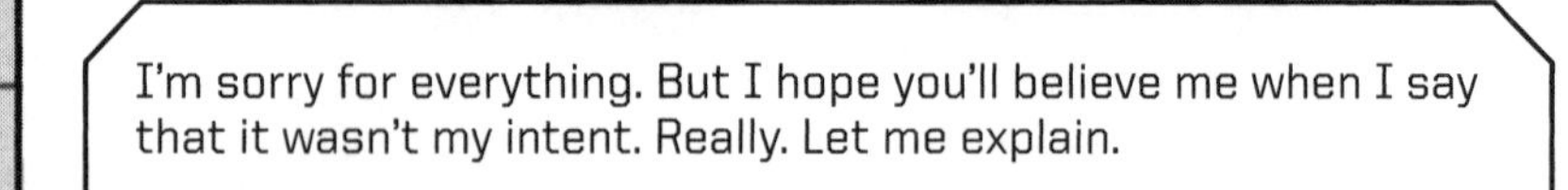
I'm sorry for everything. But I hope you'll believe me when I say that it wasn't my intent. Really. Let me explain.

With enough money, you can buy anything. So I built a time machine using some of my fortune. I only wanted to use it to make even more money, in the future, or in the past . . . wherever.

But when I activated it, it transported someone through from the 21st century. They stole my time-travel device. And I've been trying to track them ever since.

Peacekeepers Garden
!
OUR COMPUTER HAS CREATED THE FOLLOWING HOLOGRAPHIC GRID OF THE CITY, INCLUDING ALL THE SPOTS WHERE THERE HAVE BEEN ATTACKS.
ALEXIA HAS SHARED THE COORDINATES TO TRACK THE CURRENT WHEREABOUTS OF THE TIME-TRAVEL DEVICE. AND IT'S PINPOINTING ONE SPOT . . . THE DIANA PRINCE PEACEKEEPERS GARDEN.
LEGIONNAIRES, GO! AND ALEXIA, MEET US THERE.

SKRITCH
SKRATCH
PRISCILLA RICH! WHY?
I'M TIRED OF LIVING IN YOUR SHADOW. ALWAYS COMING IN SECOND. AND THEN THEY WANTED ME TO BE YOUR ORIENTATION ASSISTANT? NO WAY!
BUT WHEN ONE DOOR CLOSES, THE OTHER OPENS . . . INTO THE FUTURE.

WITH THIS DEVICE, I CAN GO ANYWHERE. MAYBE ALL THE WAY BACK TO ERASE YOU!
TIME FOR THIS CHEETAH TO RUN!
FZZZT
PLEASE TAKE IT. THE LOCATOR WILL HELP YOU TRACK HER. IT'S THE LEAST I CAN DO.
BUT YOU'LL STILL NEED TO FIND A WAY TO TRAVEL BACK IN TIME.
LEAVE THAT TO ME!

TIME PERIOD: 21ST CENTURY
LOCATION: THEMYSCIRA – PARADISE ISLAND
PROBABILITY: IF THE CHEETAH CAN STOP DIANA FROM EVER LEAVING THE ISLAND, SHE WILL NEVER GO TO SCHOOL WITH HER.

I'VE HELPED PROGRAM AND HARDWIRE YOUR LEGION BELTS TO PIGGYBACK ON THE TIME STREAM COORDINATES FROM PRISCILLA'S TIME MACHINE. WHEREVER SHE GOES, YOU'LL BE ABLE TO FOLLOW. AND ONCE YOU FIND HER, YOU CAN STOP HER, AND ULTIMATELY DESTROY HER TIME MACHINE. ONCE YOU DO THAT, IT CAN RESET THINGS BACK TO NORMAL, AS LONG AS YOU FIND A WAY TO STOP PRISCILLA FROM EVER BEING TRANSPORTED INTO THE FUTURE IN THE FIRST PLACE.

BE CAREFUL TO AVOID YOURSELVES. YOU'LL BE TRAVELING BACK IN TIME WITH THE POSSIBILITY OF CROSSING PATHS WITH YOUR DUPLICATES IN THE PAST. AVOID ANY CONTACT AT ALL COSTS.

I WILL STILL BE ABLE TO COMMUNICATE WITH YOU FROM THE COMMUNICATORS IN YOUR LEGION BELTS IF YOU REQUIRE MY HELP. AND SATURN GIRL WILL TRAVEL WITH YOU TO MAKE SURE EVERYTHING WORKS OUT.

GOOD LUCK!

– BRAINY

IT FEELS LIKE WE BARELY GOT HERE. BUT WE HAVE NO TIME TO WASTE.
BEFORE YOU GO, WE HAVE ONE LAST THING TO SHOW YOU.
HONORARY LEGION MEMBERS
EVEN THOUGH YOU CAN'T STAY, YOU'RE STILL A PART OF OUR TEAM.

BYE!
REMEMBER, WHATEVER HAPPENS, YOU MUST FOLLOW THE TIME-TRAVEL PROTOCOL.
YOU MUST WIPE THEIR MINDS FROM REMEMBERING ANY OF THESE EVENTS.
IT'S NOT RIGHT FOR THEM TO KNOW TOO MUCH ABOUT THEIR FUTURE, TO ALLOW THINGS TO HAPPEN NATURALLY.
I KNOW. IT'S JUST SAD THAT THEY WON'T REMEMBER THE HEROES THEY ARE.
BUT WE WILL.

WE MADE IT! I'M REALLY HOME! PARADISE ISLAND!
WHY WOULD YOU EVER LEAVE THIS PLACE? IT'S BEAUTIFUL.
REMIND HER TO TELL YOU LATER. RIGHT NOW, WE NEED TO FOCUS ON FINDING PRISCILLA.
THERE'S A SAFE HOUSE NEARBY IN THE JUNGLE. LET'S START THERE.
AND DON'T GET SEEN. MY SISTERS WON'T LIKE YOU.
WHAT'S NOT TO LIKE?

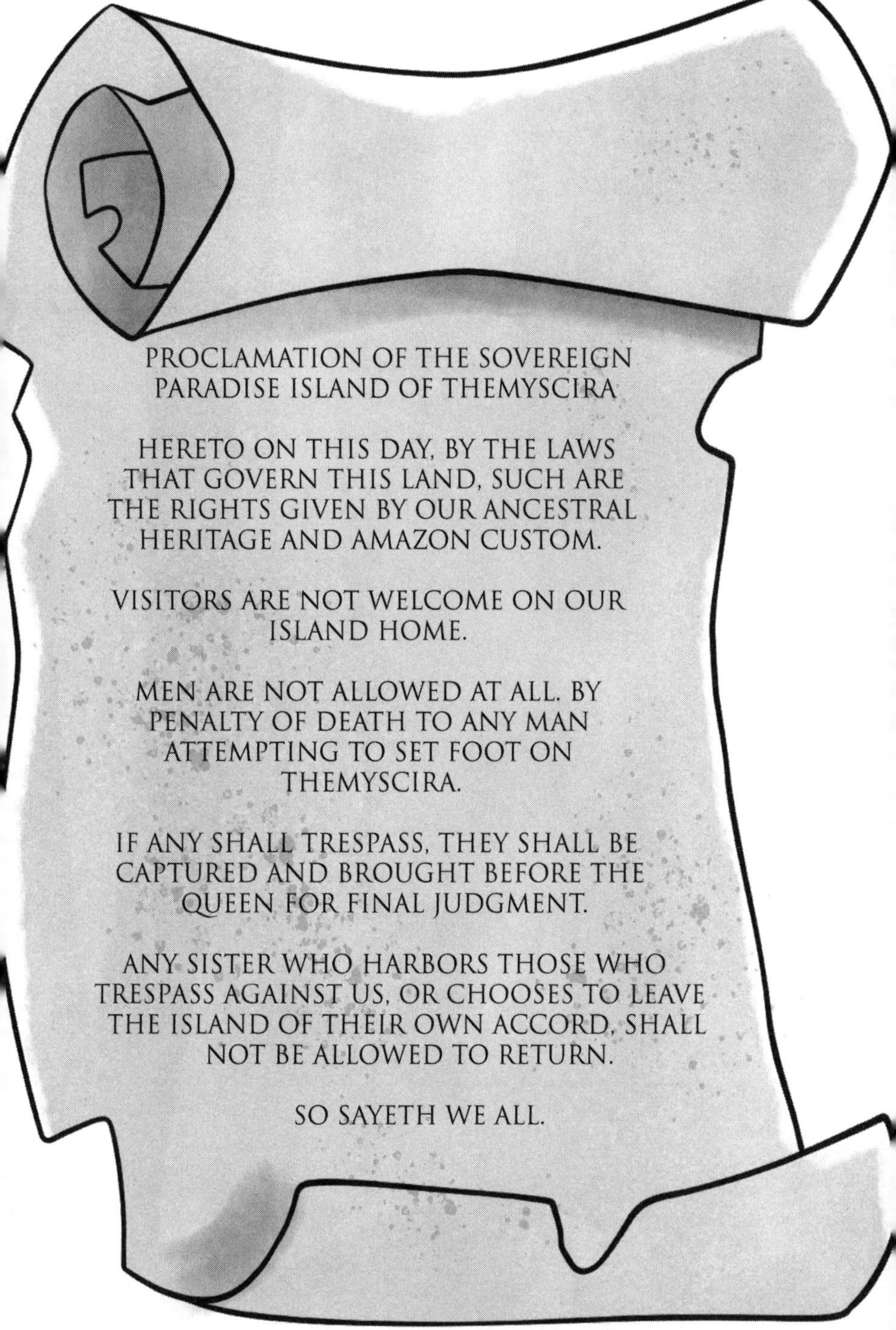

PROCLAMATION OF THE SOVEREIGN
PARADISE ISLAND OF THEMYSCIRA

HERETO ON THIS DAY, BY THE LAWS
THAT GOVERN THIS LAND, SUCH ARE
THE RIGHTS GIVEN BY OUR ANCESTRAL
HERITAGE AND AMAZON CUSTOM.

VISITORS ARE NOT WELCOME ON OUR
ISLAND HOME.

MEN ARE NOT ALLOWED AT ALL. BY
PENALTY OF DEATH TO ANY MAN
ATTEMPTING TO SET FOOT ON
THEMYSCIRA.

IF ANY SHALL TRESPASS, THEY SHALL BE
CAPTURED AND BROUGHT BEFORE THE
QUEEN FOR FINAL JUDGMENT.

ANY SISTER WHO HARBORS THOSE WHO
TRESPASS AGAINST US, OR CHOOSES TO LEAVE
THE ISLAND OF THEIR OWN ACCORD, SHALL
NOT BE ALLOWED TO RETURN.

SO SAYETH WE ALL.

THE AMAZONS OF THEMYSCIRA, AWAY FROM THE TEMPTATIONS OF MAN'S WORLD, STARTED A NEW LIFE ON THIS HIDDEN ISLAND. BLESSED BY THE OLYMPIAN GODDESSES OF ARTEMIS, ATHENA, DEMETER, HESTIA, AND APHRODITE, THE AMAZONS WERE GRANTED IMMORTALITY, GREAT PHYSICAL STRENGTH, BEAUTY, AND WISDOM. ARTISANS AND WARRIORS, THEY WISH TO LIVE A LIFE OF PEACE.
FOR CENTURIES, THE AMAZONS HAVE LIVED IN A PERFECT STATE OF HARMONY WITH THEIR SURROUNDINGS AND EACH OTHER, UNDER A THEOCRACY. THEY CELEBRATE THEIR CREATION EACH YEAR IN A FEAST OF FIVE, REMEMBERING THE GODDESSES WHO BROUGHT THEM TO LIFE.
EACH GENERATION, A CHAMPION AMBASSADOR IS CROWNED, TO LEAVE THE ISLAND AND BRING THE MERITS OF VIRTUE, LOVE, AND EQUALITY TO MAN'S WORLD.

MMMPHFFF
QUIET. THERE'S SOMEONE ELSE HERE.
PRISCILLA, IS THAT YOU?
IT'S YOU!
IT'S ME?!
WHAT'S GOING ON? WHO ARE YOU?

FIRST, I'D LIKE YOU TO TELL ME WHAT HAPPENED TO YOU.
THERE WAS A GIRL. SOMEONE I'D NEVER SEEN BEFORE. NOT FROM HERE. SHE'S THE ONE WHO TIED ME UP!
IF I MISS THE COMPETITION TODAY, I WON'T HAVE A CHANCE TO LEAVE THE ISLAND AND GO TO SCHOOL.
DON'T WORRY. YOU WON'T MISS THE COMPETITION. I'LL COMPETE FOR YOU.
BOTH OF YOU, GO WITH DIANA.
I'LL STAY HERE AND CLEAR THINGS UP WITH HER.

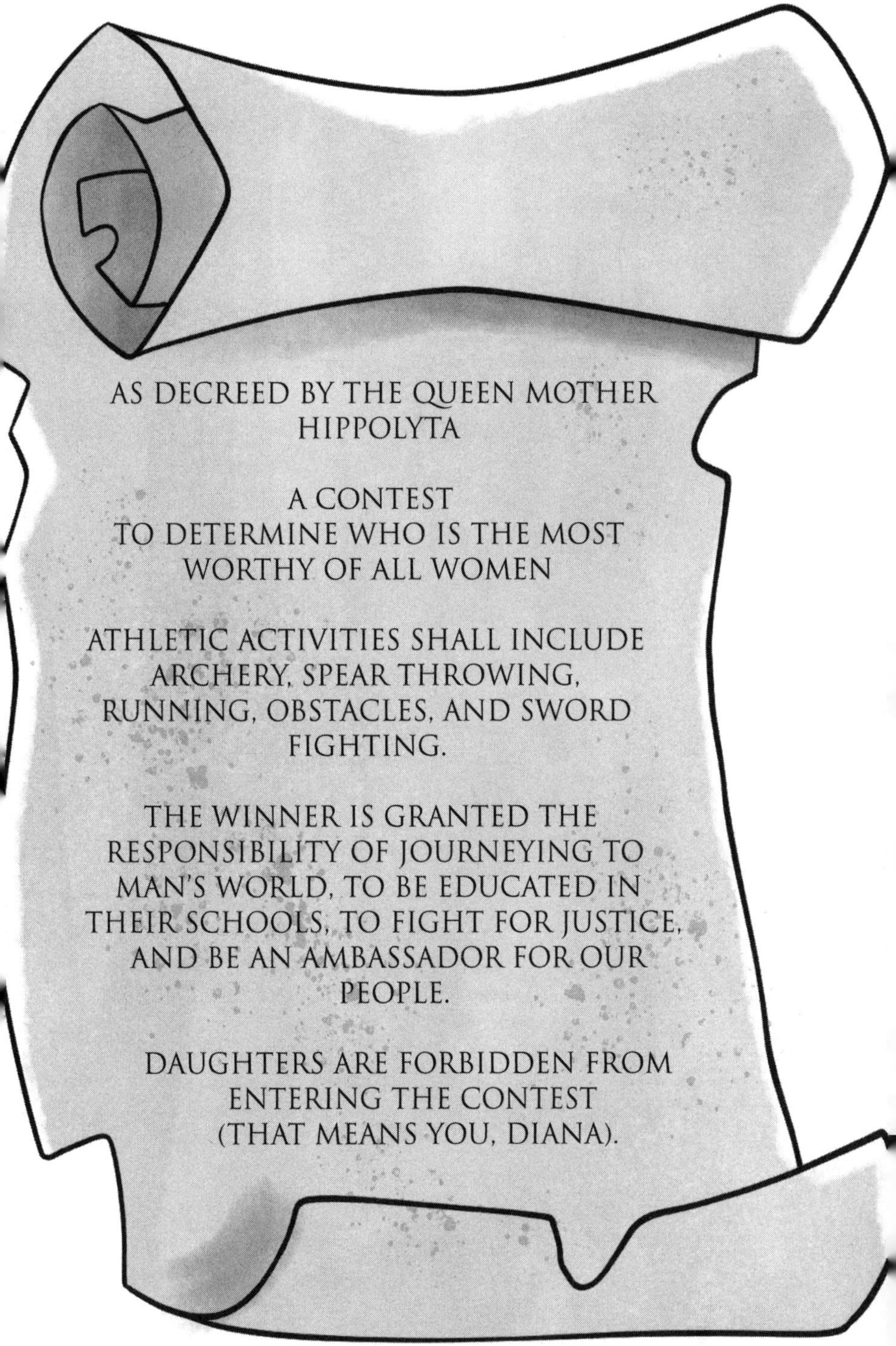

AS DECREED BY THE QUEEN MOTHER
HIPPOLYTA

A CONTEST
TO DETERMINE WHO IS THE MOST
WORTHY OF ALL WOMEN

ATHLETIC ACTIVITIES SHALL INCLUDE
ARCHERY, SPEAR THROWING,
RUNNING, OBSTACLES, AND SWORD
FIGHTING.

THE WINNER IS GRANTED THE
RESPONSIBILITY OF JOURNEYING TO
MAN'S WORLD, TO BE EDUCATED IN
THEIR SCHOOLS, TO FIGHT FOR JUSTICE,
AND BE AN AMBASSADOR FOR OUR
PEOPLE.

DAUGHTERS ARE FORBIDDEN FROM
ENTERING THE CONTEST
(THAT MEANS YOU, DIANA).

Remember, you must remain hidden during the competition
GAAAAHHHHH
A little warning next time you jump inside our heads!
No one must see you, so it doesn't upset the timeline from happening
We understand
Amazons wear armor and helmets to conceal their identities
I suggest you find some to stay hidden
Then get close enough to grab the time machine away from Priscilla if you get the chance
That's a good plan
Good luck

DIANA WINS ARCHERY
1
PRISCILLA WINS OBSTACLES
1
DIANA WINS SPEAR THROWING
PRISCILLA WINS RACE RUNNING
2
2

DATA-PAD JOURNAL ENTRY 03

DIANA PRINCE

I'VE NEVER BEEN MORE NERVOUS IN MY LIFE. AND I'VE BEEN HERE BEFORE.

THE FIRST TIME, I WAS COMPETING TO GET THE CHANCE TO LEAVE THE ISLAND AND GO TO SCHOOL. THIS TIME, I'M COMPETING IN ORDER TO STOP HISTORY BEING REWRITTEN . . . AND ERASING ME FROM IT.

THE OTHER DIFFERENCE IS I'M COMPETING AGAINST MY CLASS RIVAL. PRISCILLA AND I HAVE ALWAYS BEEN AT ODDS WITH EACH OTHER. SHE HATES ME ENOUGH TO TRY TO REWRITE MY LIFE. I DON'T KNOW HOW TO STOP SOMEONE LIKE THAT. TO CHANGE THEIR MIND ABOUT ME. TIME AND PATIENCE ARE LUXURIES I DON'T HAVE.

I JUST HOPE WHEN I COMPETE IN THE LAST EVENT TOMORROW, I CAN BEAT HER, EVEN IF SHE IS FASTER THAN ME. BECAUSE IF I DON'T, SHE MIGHT NOT STOP WITH JUST REWRITING MY HISTORY. NO ONE WILL BE ABLE TO STOP HER FROM REWRITING EVERYTHING.

AT LEAST BRUCE AND CLARK ARE HERE. THEY HAVE THEIR OWN SECRET PLAN TO GET BACK THE TIME MACHINE. WHATEVER IT IS, I HOPE IT WORKS — FOR ALL OF US.

STOP THE CHEETAH'S PLANS
1. DRESS UP LIKE AMAZONS
2. SNEAK AROUND PALACE GROUNDS
3. CLIMB TOWER WALLS
4. CRAWL INSIDE PRISCILLA'S ROOM
5. DESTROY TIME MACHINE

THIS IS THE WRONG SIZE.
IT'S NOT A FASHION SHOW. JUST PUT IT ON!
AAAACHOOOO!
FASTER! FASTER!!

ME FIRST!
I THOUGHT I WAS GOING FIRST!
CRASHH
GREAT PLAN!
RETREAT!!

How are you, Diana?
Okay
The competition is tied
A winner will be decided in the final event tomorrow
I can barely sleep up here in the tower
Try to relax and remember you've done this before
I'm still in the safe house with the other Diana
We'll continue to hide here until you win and get back the time machine
Good night

AS YOU PREPARE FOR YOUR FINAL CONTEST, MAY HERA CONTINUE TO BLESS YOU IN LIFE'S JOURNEY.
PREPARE TO DO YOUR BEST. AND MAY THE GODDESSES SHINE THEIR LIGHT UPON YOU.
- HIPPOLYTA

MAY THE FINAL CONTEST BEGIN!
I DON'T KNOW WHO YOU ARE, BUT I DIDN'T TRAVEL ALL THIS WAY TO LOSE.
HYAAAAH!
CLANGGG

CLUNK
WE HAVE A NEW CHAMPION!
AS YOUR VICTOR, I WISH TO TRAVEL TO THE OUTSIDE WORLD . . . TO GO TO SCHOOL.
DIANA?!?

BUT HOW?! I TIED YOU UP!
OR SOMEONE WHO LOOKED LIKE HER.
YOU RAN OUT OF TIME, CHEATER— CHEETAH—WHATEVER.
LET ME GO!
I THOUGHT BOYS WEREN'T ALLOWED HERE!
INTRUDERS! GET THEM!
GREAT PLAN!
RETREAT!

SATURN GIRL, I'VE FOUND WHERE PRISCILLA HAS JUMPED IN TIME NEXT. I'VE UPLOADED THE COORDINATES INTO THE LOCATOR DEVICE, AND ADJUSTED YOUR BELTS TO MAKE THE JUMP.

MAKE SURE THAT YOU'VE WIPED THE MIND OF THE OTHER DIANA SO SHE DOESN'T REMEMBER ANYTHING BEFORE YOU LEAVE. THAT WAY HISTORY CAN REMAIN INTACT.

ONCE YOU LOCATE THE OTHERS ON THE BEACH, YOU CAN SAFELY MAKE THE JUMP. THIS TIME, YOU'RE GOING INTO THE FUTURE FROM WHERE YOU ARE. BUT NOT BACK HOME.

– BRAINY

DIANA, THERE YOU ARE!
GUARDS, CONTINUE TO SEARCH FOR THE INTRUDERS.
I HAVE TO GET MY DAUGHTER PREPARED. TO GO TO SCHOOL.

DATA-PAD JOURNAL ENTRY 04
DIANA PRINCE

IT WAS INTERESTING TRAVELING BACK IN TIME TO THIS MOMENT. I HAD NO IDEA WHAT WAS IN MY FUTURE AFTER WINNING THE CONTEST THE FIRST TIME. BUT I'M THANKFUL I GOT TO WIN IT AGAIN, IF ONLY TO STOP PRISCILLA FROM REWRITING HISTORY. WE CAME SO CLOSE TO CAPTURING HER, BUT SHE MANAGED TO ESCAPE FOR THE MOMENT.

STILL, IT WAS FUN HAVING CLARK AND BRUCE ALONG TO SEE WHERE I GREW UP. MAYBE NEXT TIME THEY VISIT, THEY'LL GET A CHANCE TO ENJOY MORE OF THE ISLAND WITHOUT BEING ATTACKED. HEH HEH . . . PROBABLY NOT.

OUR NEXT TIME-TRAVEL JUMP TOOK US ALL BY SURPRISE . . .

THIS IS WHERE PRISCILLA HAS BEEN LOCATED.
BUT WHERE ARE WE?
WE'RE BACK AT SCHOOL!

SPLATT
SPLATT
SPLATT
SPLATT

HAHAHAHAHA
OH, NO.
THIS ISN'T JUSTICE PREP.
WE'VE TRAVELED BACK TO DUCARD ACADEMY!

This is your school, correct?

Yes and no

This is our original school, the evil one, before our current one

I'm not sure I understand

I guess not everything is in the history books about us

This is the school where we all first met

The principal and the students just happen to be evil.

That's it!

What?

Priscilla must be here to try to stop us from ever meeting

She was unable to stop me from coming to school

But maybe she could stop all of us from ever becoming friends

This makes things more complicated

Because now there's a much higher possibility that you can run into your duplicates here

What happens if we do?

It can destroy the space-time continuum and the universe as we know it

That only means one thing

We're going to need disguises

HOLD STILL!
I AM!
SHH! I SEE SOMETHING . . .

IT'S MR. GRUNDY, OUR HOMEROOM TEACHER.
WHERE THE THREE OF US FIRST MET.
BUT NEITHER OF YOU ARE THERE.
THERE'S TWO EMPTY SEATS NEXT TO ME IN THERE.
PRISCILLA IS ALREADY CHANGING HISTORY.

AWW . . . ARE YOU ALL BY YOURSELF?
WE'LL BE YOUR NEW FRIENDS, FOR A PRICE.
GIVE US ALL YOUR MONEY!
YES, RUN TO THE BANK! WE'LL COLLECT FROM YOU LATER!
TODAY'S BEEN HOOTS OF FUN SO FAR. FIRST CAPTURING THOSE TWO DORKS AND NOW THIS GIRL.
LET'S GO GET INTO MORE BIG TROUBLE. *HEH HEH.*
TO AVOID RUNNING INTO MYSELF, SATURN GIRL AND I WILL FOLLOW PRISCILLA'S GANG.
YOU TWO FOLLOW THE OTHER DIANA. AND FIND PRISCILLA!

MESSAGES
GROUP CHAT
is everyone there?
Here!
yes
it's good to use our cell phones again in this timeline
and better this way
no more brain headache surprises
I never felt any of those.
that's because you don't have a brain
stop it! we don't have time for this!
Right
we need to stay split up in order to cover more ground
and find Priscilla
but not get seen
SEND

MESSAGES

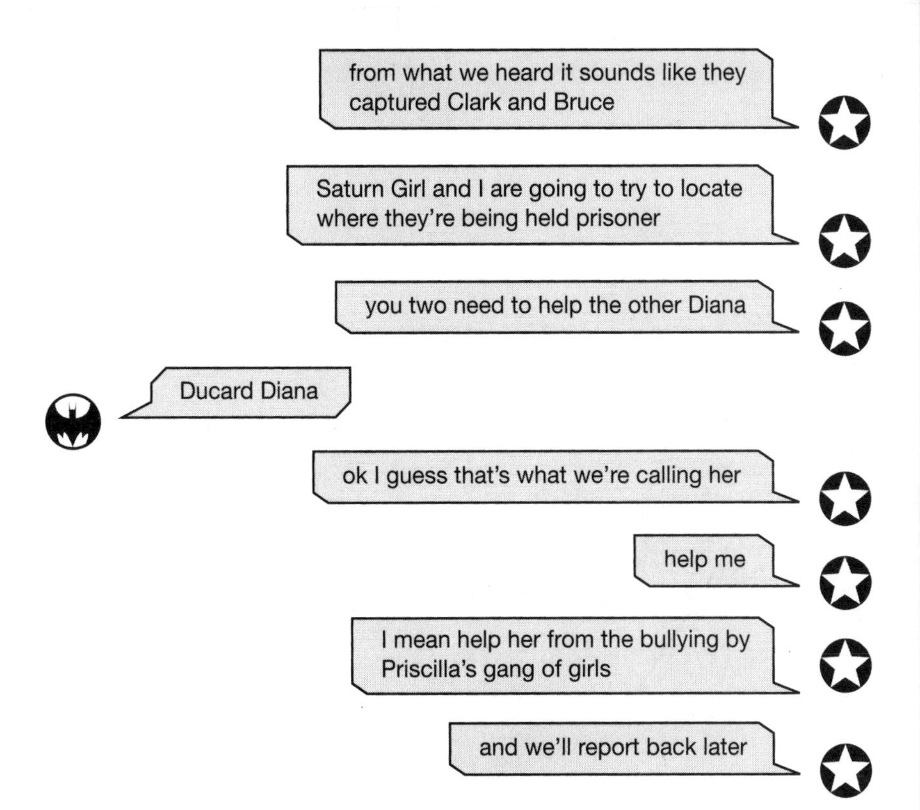

SEND

SPLAT

THERE YOU ARE! HEY, YOU'VE GOTTA PAY TO EAT HERE.
OTHERWISE THERE'S MORE A THAT COMIN'.
REMEMBER, IT'S BEST TO AVOID BEING SEEN.
WE SHOULD DO SOMETHING.
WE NEED TO AVOID BEING SEEN. JUST WATCH, FOR NOW.

I'll track their movements, and when no one is around, I'll spring a trap.

I can talk to them from above. They'll just hear my voice as a warning.

I've got traps set up all over school. We can monitor them back in the cave.

Using my super-speed, I can just tie their shoes together so they keep tripping. And they'll never see me do it.

I can interrogate them my way.

Or I can approach them my way.

DUE TO COMPUTER DAMAGE
AND SECURITY CAMERA
MALFUNCTION
THE SCHOOL LIBRARY WILL
BE CLOSED
ON FRIDAY, SEPTEMBER 12
FOR MAINTENANCE
WE ARE SORRY FOR THIS
INCONVENIENCE

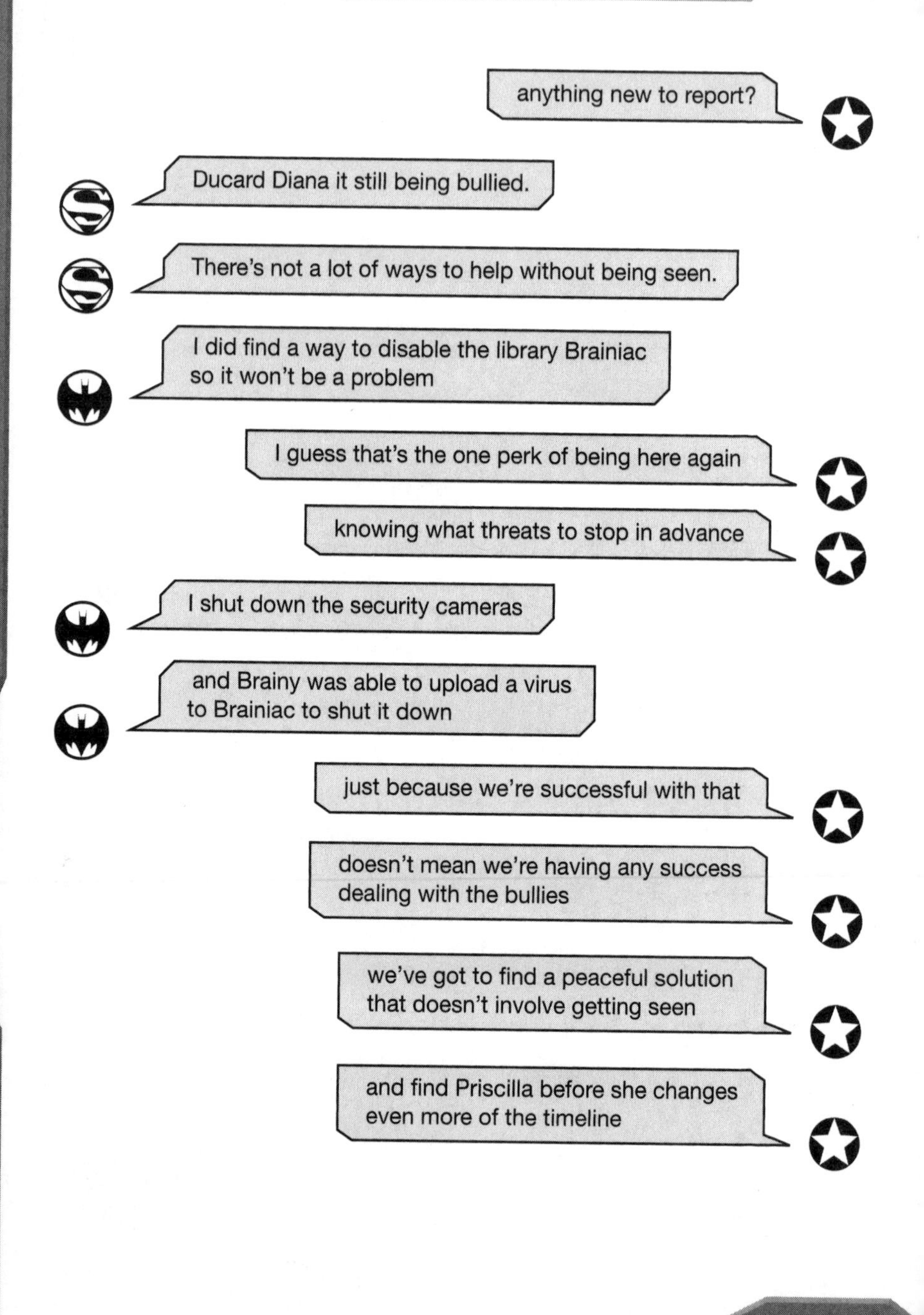
MESSAGES
GROUP CHAT
anything new to report?
Ducard Diana it still being bullied.
There's not a lot of ways to help without being seen.
I did find a way to disable the library Brainiac so it won't be a problem
I guess that's the one perk of being here again
knowing what threats to stop in advance
I shut down the security cameras
and Brainy was able to upload a virus to Brainiac to shut it down
just because we're successful with that
doesn't mean we're having any success dealing with the bullies
we've got to find a peaceful solution that doesn't involve getting seen
and find Priscilla before she changes even more of the timeline
SEND

WHERE ARE WE?
THE STUDENT DORMS.
I NEVER KNEW THESE EXISTED.
NOT EVERYONE IS ABLE TO LIVE AT HOME WHILE GOING TO SCHOOL.
SINCE DIANA WAS AN EXCHANGE STUDENT, SHE LIVED ON CAMPUS.
WHAT EVIL GOES ON INSIDE THERE?
WE'LL NEVER KNOW. IT'S A GIRLS-ONLY DORM.
DEFINITELY EVIL.

THERE SHE IS. GET HER!
I'LL HANDLE THIS.
LOOK OUT!
SLAM

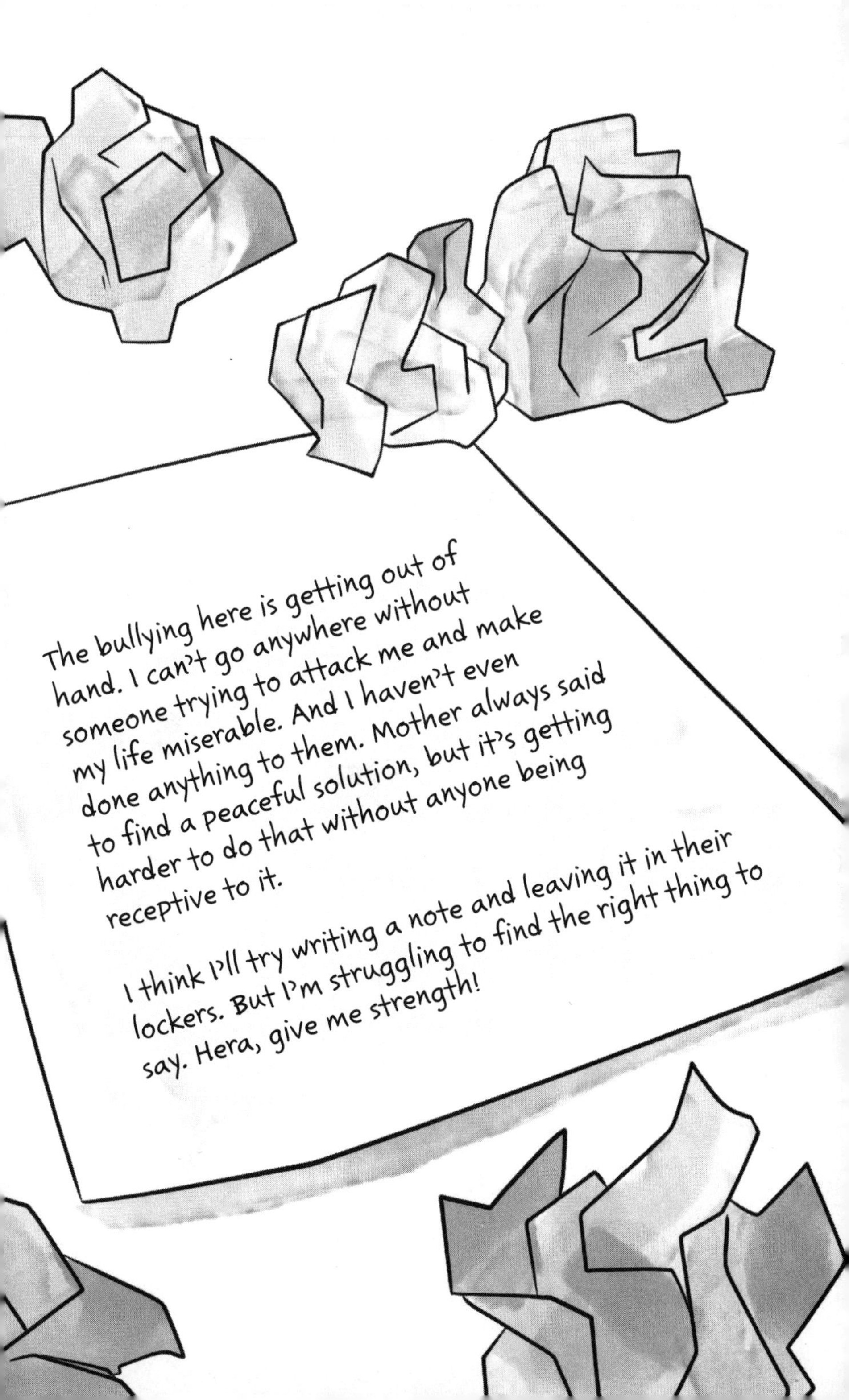

The bullying here is getting out of hand. I can't go anywhere without someone trying to attack me and make my life miserable. And I haven't even done anything to them. Mother always said to find a peaceful solution, but it's getting harder to do that without anyone being receptive to it.

I think I'll try writing a note and leaving it in their lockers. But I'm struggling to find the right thing to say. Hera, give me strength!

NAME: BWAYNE
TO: CKENT, DPRINCE
SUBJECT: (FWD) DIANA JOURNAL

I WAS ABLE TO HACK INTO DUCARD DIANA'S EMAIL ACCOUNT AND FOUND THIS JOURNAL ENTRY. TROUBLE IS COMING. SO I THOUGHT YOU ALL SHOULD READ IT.

– BRUCE

< < < < < < < < < < < < < < < < < < < < < < <
< <

RE: JOURNAL ENTRY

I TRIED THE PEACEFUL SOLUTION. TRIED TO WRITE NOTES TO THE ONES BULLYING ME. BUT BEFORE I WAS ABLE TO SEND THE NOTES OUT, THEY BROKE INTO MY DORM ROOM AND DESTROYED IT.

I'M DONE WITH THE PEACEFUL APPROACH. NO MORE DIPLOMATIC SOLUTIONS. BOYS AREN'T THE ONLY ONES WHO SEEM BAD IN THIS WORLD. THE GIRLS CAN BE JUST AS MEAN TO ONE ANOTHER, TOO.

I'VE BEEN TRYING TO HOLD MY TEMPER BUT I'VE HAD ENOUGH. IF THEY WANT A FIGHT, I'LL GIVE IT TO THEM. THEY HAVE NO IDEA WHO THEY'RE DEALING WITH!

SCHOOL NURSE INCIDENT REPORT

STUDENT: Harleen Quinzel, Circe, Doris Zeul, Louise Lincoln

TEACHER: unlisted

CLASS: unlisted

DATE: September 19

DESCRIPTION OF THE INCIDENT:

When I arrived at school today, many injured students were waiting in the hallway to see me: one with a fractured arm from being stuffed into a trash can, others with bumps and bruises. Some claim they were forced to tell the truth, but weren't sure how they were coerced. And others have stained clothes and matted hair from a cafeteria food fight.

ACTION TAKEN:

Most students were administered light first aid treatments of bandages or referred to the school guidance counselor to share their feelings.

FURTHER RECOMMENDED CARE:

None at this time. Although if this keeps up, you might want to hire additional staff to help in the school nurse office. I'm not a hospital or clinic, you know!

IF YOU HAVE ANY QUESTIONS ABOUT THIS EVENT, PLEASE CALL THE NURSE'S OFFICE.

WELCOME TO YOUR INTRO TO LITERATURE CLASS, AS TAUGHT BY ME.
YOU MAY CALL ME MR. TETCH. I'D EVEN PREFER THE MAD HATTER.
THAT BOOK IS A FAIRY TALE. IT'S NOT REAL.
AND YET ALL OF YOU ARE VERY REAL TO ME, ALICE.
YOU ARE ALL MY ALICES.

DUCARD ACADEMY
TEACHER LEAVE REQUEST FORM

TEACHER NAME: Jervis Tetch
SUBJECT MATTER TAUGHT: English Literature
DATE(S) REQUESTED: Immediate

PLEASE EXPLAIN THE REASON FOR THE REQUEST:

I am unable to get my students to listen to me or do what I tell them. I need more time away to continue my development of new methods to control the minds of others. Or I will certainly go mad.

One student in particular stands out as trouble. Her name is Diana Prince. She continues to mock me, prank me, and rile the rest of the students against me. She is a belligerent ignoramus and not worthy of this learning institution. I suggest her removal from this class, removal from this school, or removal from this district. I hope that by bringing this to the attention of our school principal, he might find a spot better suited for her.

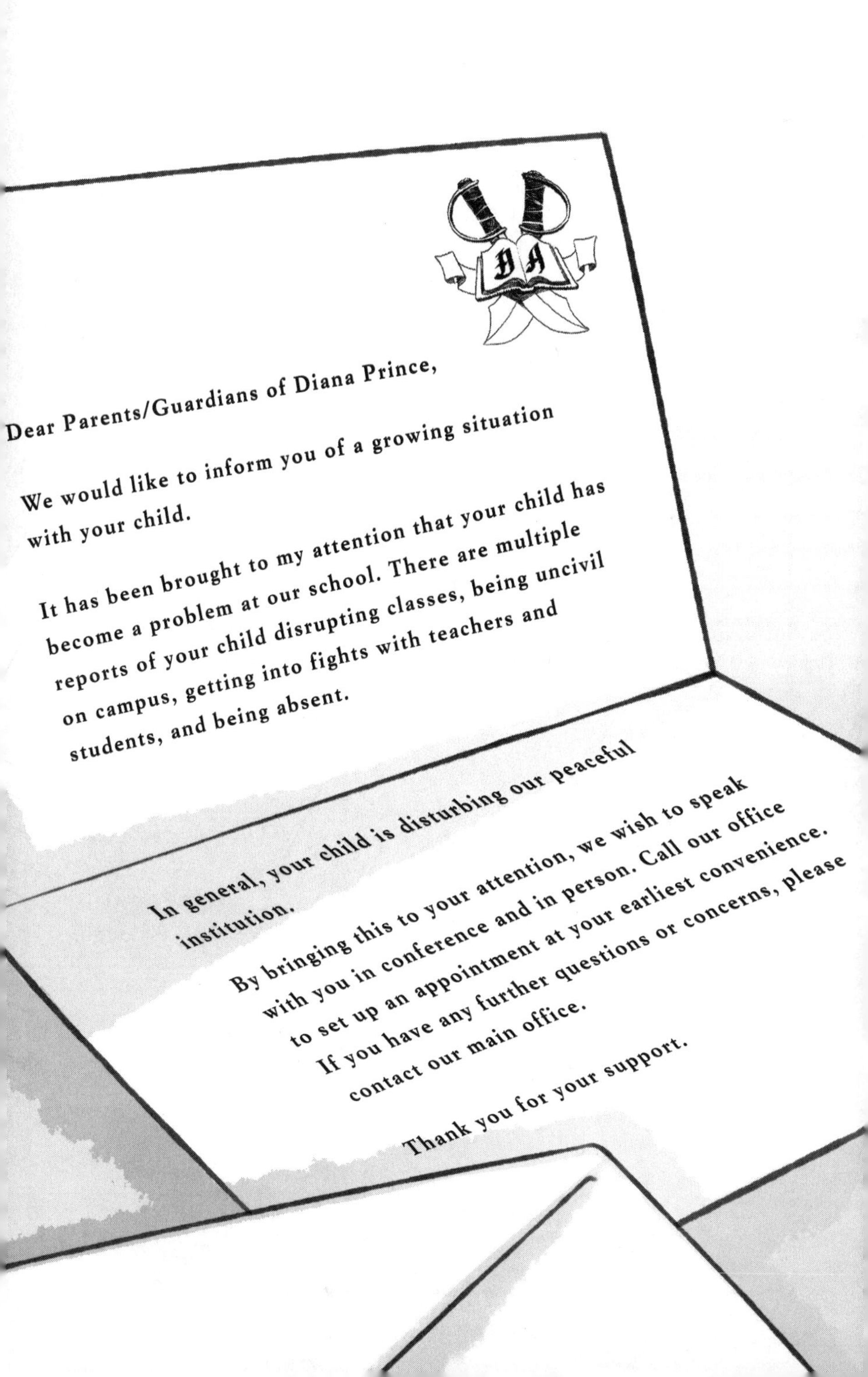

Dear Parents/Guardians of Diana Prince,

We would like to inform you of a growing situation with your child.

It has been brought to my attention that your child has become a problem at our school. There are multiple reports of your child disrupting classes, being uncivil on campus, getting into fights with teachers and students, and being absent.

In general, your child is disturbing our peaceful institution.

By bringing this to your attention, we wish to speak with you in conference and in person. Call our office to set up an appointment at your earliest convenience. If you have any further questions or concerns, please contact our main office.

Thank you for your support.

SO WHAT ARE YOU IN FOR?
FOUGHT A BUNCH OF NINJAS.
IT LOOKS LIKE YOU LOST.
YEAH . . .
HOW ABOUT YOU?
TEACHING BULLIES A LESSON.
ARE YOU A BULLY?
NO!
THAT'S WHAT I THOUGHT.

IT WAS REQUESTED I COME SEE MY DAUGHTER.
YOU MUST BE DIANA'S MOM. IT MUST BE NICE LIVING ON AN ISLAND AWAY FROM ALL THIS.
YOU HAVE NO IDEA.
THE TROUBLEMAKER IS OVER THERE AGAINST THE WALL.
WE TRIED TO RESTRAIN HER, BUT SHE KEPT BREAKING OUT OF HER ROPES AND CHAINS. I WISH I WERE KIDDING.
I NEVER EXPECTED TO FIND YOU HERE. OR HEAR THE THINGS SAID ABOUT YOU.
WHAT CAN I SAY? THIS IS WHAT "PEACE" LOOKS LIKE, MOTHER.
IT WAS AGAINST MY JUDGMENT TO ALLOW YOU TO COME TO THIS SCHOOL.
BUT IF THIS IS HOW THE WORLD IS, IT'S EVEN WORSE THAN I THOUGHT. HERA, HELP ME.
YOUR MOM'S NICE.

MESSAGES

GROUP CHAT

SEND

I WANT TO TRY OUT FOR THE TEAM.
YOU'RE IN!!
AS CAPTAIN, LET ME WELCOME YOU TO THE TEAM
I DIDN'T JUST ERASE THE OLD DIANA. I REMADE HER AS BAD AS THE REST OF US.
MY NEW BFF . . . BEST FRENEMY FOREVER!!

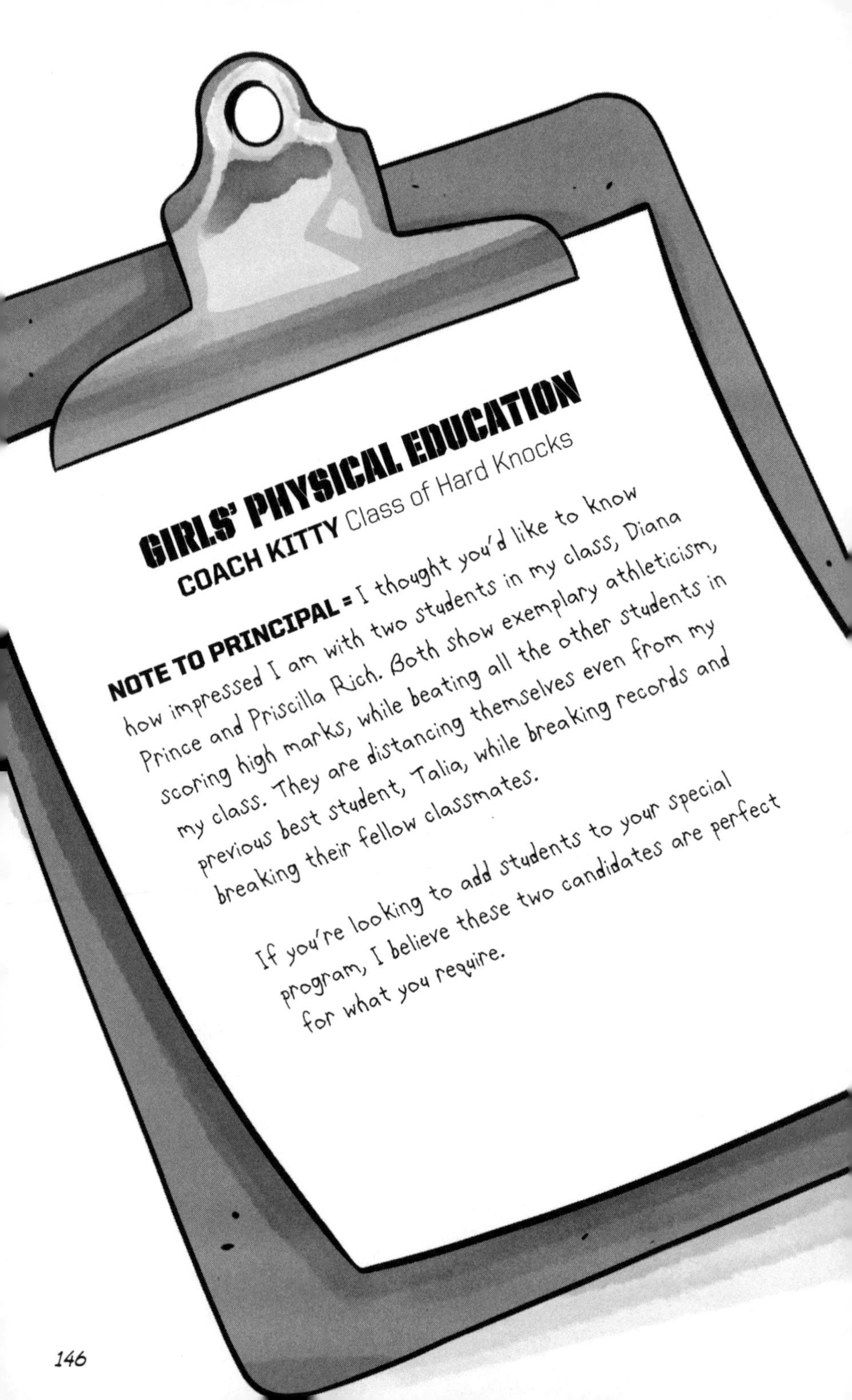
GIRLS' PHYSICAL EDUCATION
COACH KITTY Class of Hard Knocks

NOTE TO PRINCIPAL = I thought you'd like to know how impressed I am with two students in my class, Diana Prince and Priscilla Rich. Both show exemplary athleticism, scoring high marks, while beating all the other students in my class. They are distancing themselves even from my previous best student, Talia, while breaking records and breaking their fellow classmates.

If you're looking to add students to your special program, I believe these two candidates are perfect for what you require.

STUDENT EVALUATION REPORT

STUDENT: Diana Prince **PROFESSOR:** Hugo Strange

Which of the following best describes you?
Choose only one:

❑ Ambitious ☒ Angry ❑ Bored ❑ Calm ❑ Confused ❑ Creative ❑ Embarrassed
❑ Excited ❑ Focused ❑ Happy ❑ Hungry ❑ Lonely ❑ Loved ❑ Patient
❑ Proud ❑ Relieved ❑ Sad ❑ Scared ❑ Surprised ❑ Tired ❑ Other

Please rate the following based on how you are feeling about each area of your life:

Friendships
Terrible — Great
1 2 3 4 5 6 (7) 8 9 10

Home/Family
Terrible — Great
1 2 (3) 4 5 6 7 8 9 10

Grades/School
Terrible — Great
1 2 3 (4) 5 6 7 8 9 10

Diagnosis:

As a foreign exchange student, Diana should struggle to fit in and belong. But she's really tapped into her temper and anger and is getting everything she wants. No one bullies her anymore. No one challenges her. She has no true friends besides the other bullies that she's scared into submission. Even the teachers are afraid of her. I feared she might be too hard to break and too tough to handle. But she's proved me wrong.

Special Notes:

She's exactly who we want. A perfect candidate for the Nanda Parbat program. It is time for her to meet the principal. Just don't hold it against her that she's scoring higher than your daughter in athletics.

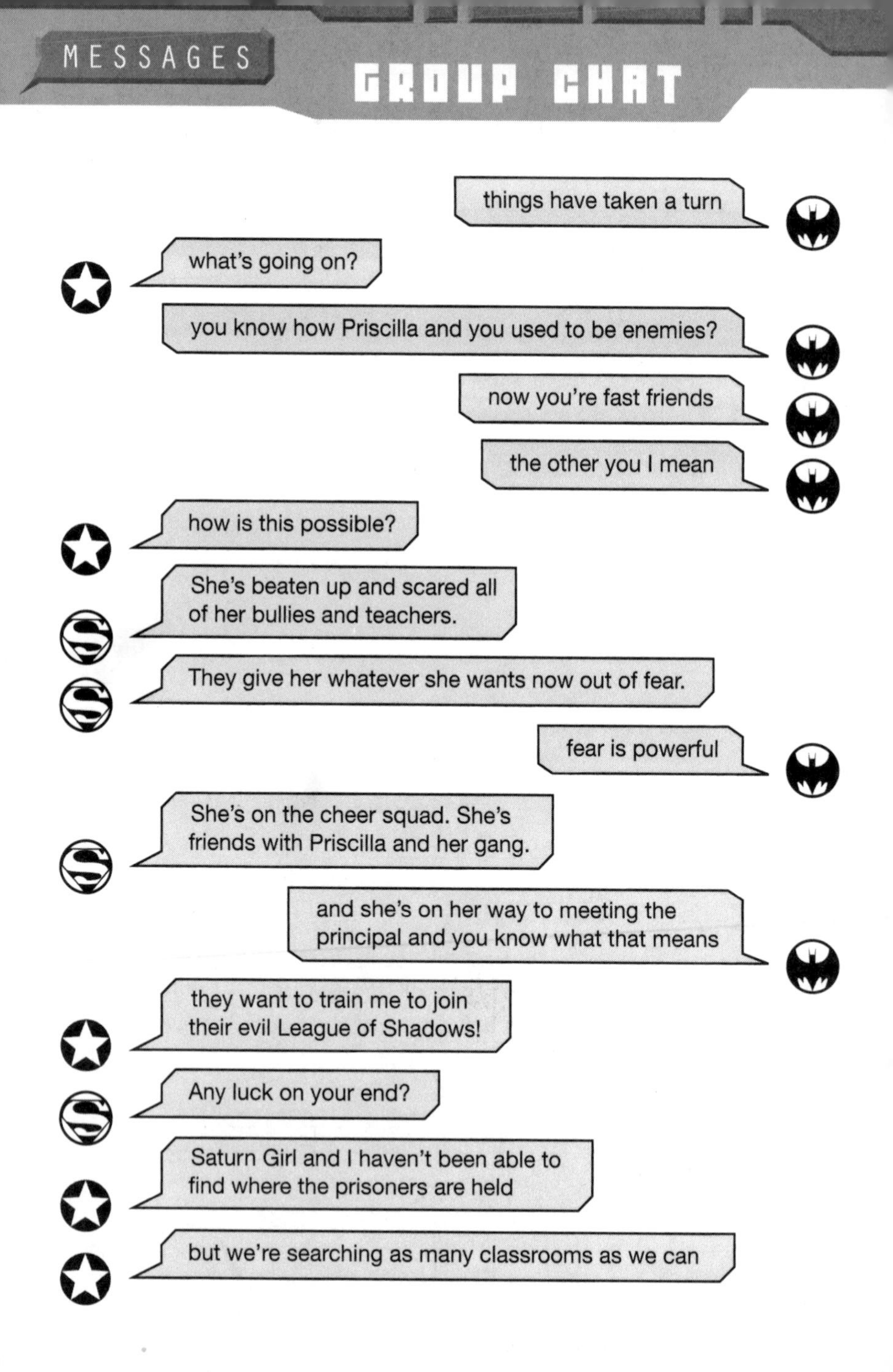
MESSAGES
GROUP CHAT
things have taken a turn
what's going on?
you know how Priscilla and you used to be enemies?
now you're fast friends
the other you I mean
how is this possible?
She's beaten up and scared all of her bullies and teachers.
They give her whatever she wants now out of fear.
fear is powerful
She's on the cheer squad. She's friends with Priscilla and her gang.
and she's on her way to meeting the principal and you know what that means
they want to train me to join their evil League of Shadows!
Any luck on your end?
Saturn Girl and I haven't been able to find where the prisoners are held
but we're searching as many classrooms as we can
SEND

HALLOWEEN IS GREAT!
WE DON'T EVEN HAVE TO HIDE ANYMORE, SINCE NO ONE EVEN CARES OR KNOWS WHO WE ARE.
HOLD UP!
IT'S OUR DUPLICATES, REMEMBER? THIS IS THE MOMENT WHEN WE FIRST REVEALED OUR SUPER HERO IDENTITIES TO ONE ANOTHER.
COME ON. WE NEED TO STAY AWAY FROM THEM.
BUT I DO KNOW SOMEONE WE SHOULD SEE.

TALIA . . . WE NEED TO TALK.
DO I KNOW YOU?
IT DOESN'T MATTER. ALL YOU NEED TO KNOW IS THAT PRISCILLA AND DIANA ARE TRYING TO TAKE OVER THE SCHOOL, AND BUMP YOU OFF AS YOUR FATHER'S FAVORITE.
WHO ARE YOU? WHAT ARE YOU TALKING ABOUT?
IT'S THEM! THEY'RE OVER THERE!
LOOK, WE KNOW EVERYTHING.
YOU'RE THE DAUGHTER OF THE PRINCIPAL, WHO IS RĀ'S AL GHŪL, AND HE'S TRAINING NEW ASSASSINS FOR HIS LEAGUE, ***BLAH BLAH BLAH.***
I HAVE NO IDEA WHAT YOU'RE TALKING ABOUT.
SNAP
DISPOSE OF THEM.

TIRED OF WORKING ALONE TO RULE THE WORLD?

SEEKING A GROUP TO DO IT WITH?

LET'S GANG TOGETHER AND COME UP WITH THE SOLUTION.

MEET IN THE LIBRARY AFTER SCHOOL AND JOIN OUR "CHEETAH PACK"!

I'M GLAD YOU ACCEPTED THE INVITATION.
WELCOME TO THE "CHEETAH PACK"! MY ALL-GIRL GANG.
WHAT'S OUR PURPOSE HERE?
TO TAKE OVER THE SCHOOL, OF COURSE.
AND I HAVE JUST THE WAY TO DO IT.
I'M GOING TO RUN FOR CLASS PRESIDENT. AND YOU'RE GOING TO HELP ME WIN.

THE CAT IS OUT OF THE BAG!
PRISCILLA
FOR
CLASS PRESIDENT

The claws come out!

Boys ruin everything.
It's time for a girl to lead.

Lex tries to buy the election.

Money can't buy everything.

Say mrreow to your new
class president!

LETTER FROM THE PRESIDENT by Priscilla Rich

You don't have to have money to win an election, but it doesn't hurt to be Rich . . . Priscilla Rich! Thank you for your vote. As your new class president, I'm going to hit the ground running. I ran this race as fast as I could, and now I want to do the same for this school. All of you are part of my "Cheetah Pack" now (girls, anyways). It's time for us to control this school and our future. And it's my promise that we'll get everything we want . . . everything I want. And I have all the time to do it. Thank you!

THE RULES ARE SIMPLE. PIN YOUR OPPONENT TO THE MAT, BY ANY MEANS NECESSARY.
YOU'RE GOING DOWN, DADDY'S GIRL!
THE ONLY ONE DOWN IS YOU ON YOUR BACK!
THOMP
HUH?!

WE HAVE A PIN!
I HEAR YOU'VE EXCELLED IN YOUR ATHLETICS AND STUDIES.
TODAY YOU EVEN BESTED MY DAUGHTER. A RARE AND WORTHY ACCOMPLISHMENT!
YOU'VE EARNED THIS MEDAL. AND MY ADMIRATION.
AND I'D LIKE TO OFFER YOU SOMETHING ELSE. BOTH OF YOU.
WHAT DO YOU KNOW ABOUT THE LEAGUE?

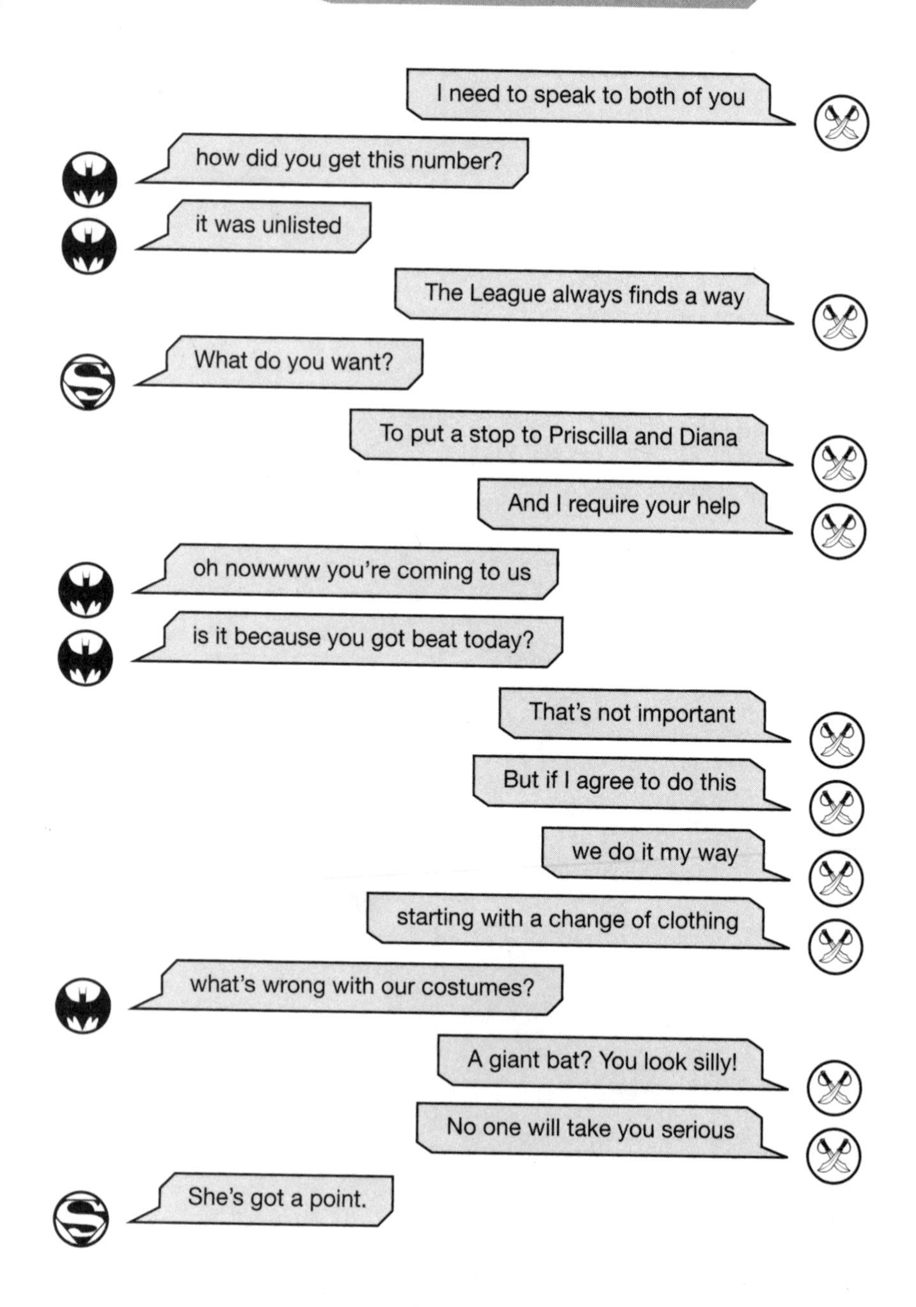
MESSAGES
GROUP CHAT
I need to speak to both of you
how did you get this number?
it was unlisted
The League always finds a way
What do you want?
To put a stop to Priscilla and Diana
And I require your help
oh nowwww you're coming to us
is it because you got beat today?
That's not important
But if I agree to do this
we do it my way
starting with a change of clothing
what's wrong with our costumes?
A giant bat? You look silly!
No one will take you serious
She's got a point.
SEND

We've been unable to reach Diana on her phone
Is everything all right?
She's decided to get answers for herself directly
She went off on her own and I lost her
Keep trying to find her
In the meantime, we've found some extra help ourselves
It's time for us to go
Keep us updated

I CAN'T WAIT ANYMORE. I KNOW YOU CAPTURED TWO BOYS. TELL ME WHERE THEY ARE!
DON'T HURT US. THEY'RE UP THERE.
AND WHERE ARE YOU SNEAKING AWAY TO?
DIANA! THERE YOU ARE.
FOLLOW ME. THE PRISONERS ARE UPSTAIRS.

THIS IS ONE HECKUVA CLUB MEETING!
IS THIS THE INITIATION?
TALIA! HOW ARE YOU INVOLVED IN ALL OF THIS?
I'LL LET MY NINJAS DO THE TALKING FOR ME.
STOP! IT'S ME, CLARK, AND BRUCE, TOO! TALIA WAS HELPING US CATCH PRISCILLA.
WHY ARE YOU DRESSED LIKE THAT?
NOT BY CHOICE! THIS IS EMBARRASSING.

FAREWELL, MY BELOVED DUCARD SCHOOL.
IT'S TIME FOR FATHER AND ME TO ESCAPE FROM THIS CRAZY PLACE!
YOU'RE NOT LEAVING BEFORE I GET ANSWERS.
I WANT THE TRUTH ABOUT WHY YOU'RE DOING ALL THIS, PRISCILLA!

DATA-PAD JOURNAL ENTRY 05
DIANA PRINCE

AFTER JUMPING ALL THROUGHOUT TIME, INTO THE FUTURE AND THE PAST, WE WERE FINALLY ABLE TO CATCH UP TO PRISCILLA. AND USING MY LASSO OF TRUTH, I WAS FINALLY ABLE TO GET AN HONEST ANSWER ABOUT WHY SHE WAS INVOLVED.

PRISCILLA HATES COMING IN SECOND EVERY TIME WE COMPETE. SHE HATES THAT I SCORE HIGHER ON TESTS, WIN MORE ATHLETIC EVENTS, HAVE MORE TRUE FRIENDS, AND THAT I'M THE ORIENTATION LEADER WHILE SHE'S ONLY MY ASSISTANT.

JEALOUSY IS THE REASON SHE HATES ME SO MUCH. AND I HAD NO IDEA UNTIL SHE TOLD ME.

I NEVER WANTED TO MAKE HER MY ENEMY. AND ANY COMPETITION WE'VE HAD, I ALWAYS CONSIDERED FUN AND INNOCENT. BUT IT'S MADE ME RETHINK HOW OTHERS FEEL. JUST BECAUSE I'M NOT CLOSE TO SOMEONE DOESN'T MEAN I CAN'T EMPATHIZE WITH THEM. I NEVER MEANT HER ANY HARM, AND I'M SORRY SHE TOOK IT THAT WAY.

TIRED OF LIVING IN MY SHADOW, SHE DITCHED ORIENTATION AND SCHOOL AS SOON AS THE TIME PORTAL OPENED UP. CLIMBING INSIDE, IT BROUGHT HER TO A FUTURE WITHOUT ME, BUT IN SOME WAYS, HISTORY STILL CAUGHT UP WITH HER. SHE TRIED TO DESTROY ANY PROOF OF MY EXISTENCE, BUT LUCKILY WE WERE ABLE TO STOP HER.

NOW THERE'S ONLY ONE THING LEFT TO DO. WE NEED TO COMPLETELY RESTORE THE TIMELINE, GO BACK TO THE MOMENT BEFORE PRISCILLA LEFT, AND STOP HER FROM GOING INTO THE FUTURE. IF WE DO THAT, WE CAN CLOSE THIS TIME LOOP AND STOP IT FROM EVER HAPPENING.

WHEN I ASKED HER WHERE THE TIME PORTAL OPENED, SHE SAID IT WAS NEAR THE GIRLS' LOCKER ROOM. SO MAYBE THERE'S STILL ENOUGH TIME TO MAKE THIS RIGHT.

I HAVE YOUR COORDINATES. IT SHOULD TAKE US DIRECTLY BEFORE THE MOMENT WHERE PRISCILLA FOUND THE TIME PORTAL INTO THE FUTURE.
LET'S GO!
WHY SHOULD I BE DIANA'S ASSISTANT? I SHOULD BE THE ORIENTATION LEADER!
FORGET HER. I'M GONNA GO CHECK THAT OUT INSTEAD.
PRISCILLA. I AM WIPING YOUR MIND OF MEMORY OF THIS INCIDENT.
WHEN I AM DONE, YOU WILL FORGET EVERYTHING THAT HAPPENED AND GO JOIN THE ORIENTATION.
BEEP

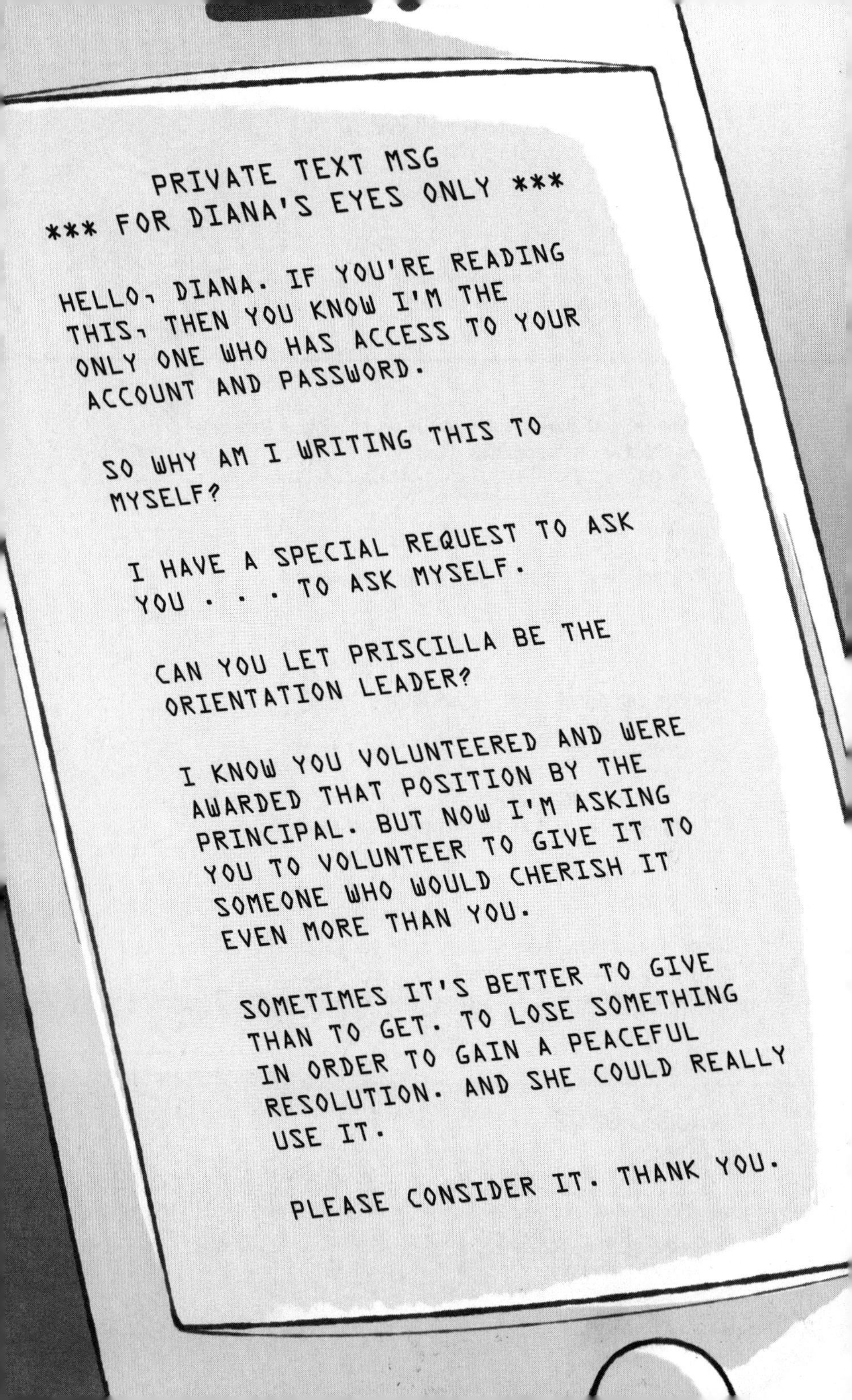

PRIVATE TEXT MSG
*** FOR DIANA'S EYES ONLY ***

HELLO, DIANA. IF YOU'RE READING THIS, THEN YOU KNOW I'M THE ONLY ONE WHO HAS ACCESS TO YOUR ACCOUNT AND PASSWORD.

SO WHY AM I WRITING THIS TO MYSELF?

I HAVE A SPECIAL REQUEST TO ASK YOU . . . TO ASK MYSELF.

CAN YOU LET PRISCILLA BE THE ORIENTATION LEADER?

I KNOW YOU VOLUNTEERED AND WERE AWARDED THAT POSITION BY THE PRINCIPAL. BUT NOW I'M ASKING YOU TO VOLUNTEER TO GIVE IT TO SOMEONE WHO WOULD CHERISH IT EVEN MORE THAN YOU.

SOMETIMES IT'S BETTER TO GIVE THAN TO GET. TO LOSE SOMETHING IN ORDER TO GAIN A PEACEFUL RESOLUTION. AND SHE COULD REALLY USE IT.

PLEASE CONSIDER IT. THANK YOU.

Normally I would have to adhere to time-travel protocol
To wipe the minds of everyone in order to preserve their future
But since you were successful in stopping Priscilla from going to the future this time
It erased that event from ever happening
There's no mind wipe necessary
Brainy will explain it all to you before you forget
Since this is the last time I talk to all of you, let me say it's been an honor getting to meet the heroes I've always looked up to
You didn't disappoint
See you in the future

NORMALLY WHEN THE TIMELINE IS RESTORED, EVERYONE WOULD BE ERASED IN THE PROCESS, AS IF IT NEVER HAPPENED. BUT I'VE BEEN ABLE TO DELAY THAT SLIGHTLY BY ACTIVATING A TIME DISPLACEMENT FIELD GENERATED BY YOUR BELTS.

YOU ALL HAVE A MOMENT TO BE OBSERVERS AND WATCH THE RESULT OF YOUR HEROIC ACHIEVEMENT WITHOUT BEING SEEN. AND THIS BRIEFEST OF MOMENTS FOR ME TO THANK YOU AS WELL.

YOU REALLY ARE HEROES!

ONCE YOU PRESS YOUR BELTS, IT WILL DEACTIVATE YOUR TIME DISPLACEMENT FIELDS, AND YOU'LL DISAPPEAR AS THE TIMELINE IS RESTORED.

THANKS FOR EVERYTHING!

- BRAINY

DING
YOU HAVE A
PRIVATE MESSAGE

PRINCIPAL-STUDENT REQUEST FORM

Student: DIANA PRINCE

RE: ORIENTATION LEADER

Thank you for awarding me the position of student orientation leader. But upon further review, I'd like to make a request that Priscilla Rich be given that position instead.

I've noticed she's never been thought of for positions like this, and I'd like to change that. As a quick learner and just quick in general, she'd be great at running the new students around campus and assisting them. Even better . . . I know that she's interested!

I'd still be happy to help as her assistant. But I look forward to her taking on the role of the new student orientation leader.

Sincerely,

Diana

QUICK ANNOUNCEMENT. I AM NO LONGER YOUR ORIENTATION LEADER.
AND THAT'S OKAY. BECAUSE I KNOW SOMEONE WHO WILL DO IT EVEN BETTER.
SO LET ME INTRODUCE YOU TO PRISCILLA RICH, YOUR NEW STUDENT ORIENTATION LEADER.
WELL, THERE'S LOTS TO SEE, SO LET'S GET RUNNING!

THAT WAS A VERY NICE THING YOU DID.
WHAT DO YOU MEAN?
YOU WERE SET FOR THAT JOB, BUT I SAW THE PAPERWORK IN THE OFFICE. I'M A BIT OF A SNOOP.
YOU GAVE IT UP SO SHE COULD HAVE IT.
CONSOLATION PRIZE. HERE'S SOME RED LICORICE.
DOESN'T SEEM FAIR NOW, DOES IT?
IT'S PERFECT.
I'M ETTA CANDY.
OF COURSE YOU ARE. AND I'M DIANA.

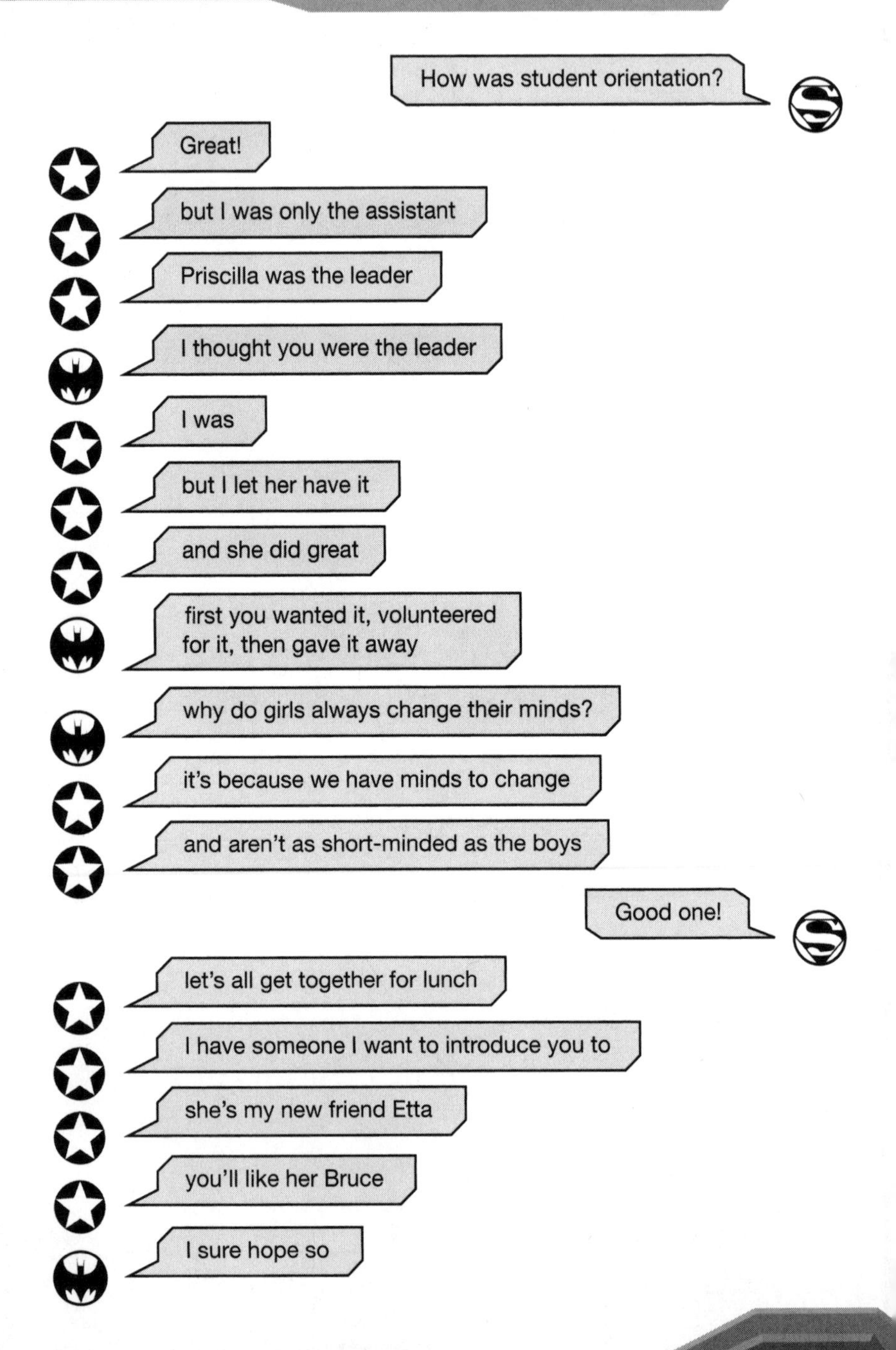
MESSAGES
GROUP CHAT
How was student orientation?
Great!
but I was only the assistant
Priscilla was the leader
I thought you were the leader
I was
but I let her have it
and she did great
first you wanted it, volunteered for it, then gave it away
why do girls always change their minds?
it's because we have minds to change
and aren't as short-minded as the boys
Good one!
let's all get together for lunch
I have someone I want to introduce you to
she's my new friend Etta
you'll like her Bruce
I sure hope so
SEND

DIANA'S JOURNAL

My mother and my sisters back home believe the best way to find a solution to a problem is through peace.

I took some recent advice and decided to do something nice for someone who hasn't always been nice to me. Even if it wasn't something I wanted or needed to do, it did change the outlook for someone else. And maybe even smooth things over. A first step toward peace.

Someone once told me, whenever she's in doubt of her own abilities, to repeat what she said . . .

I believe in Wonder Woman.

Because I believe in Diana.

Hello, my daughter. I'm so happy to hear that you're doing well in school and as a great ambassador to the world. Study hard, be at peace, and keep up the great work!

Love, Mom

PS No matter how many times you ask, boys are never allowed to visit the island. EVER! They're nothing but trouble. x o x o

Derek Fridolfs

Derek Fridolfs is a *New York Times* bestselling writer. With Dustin Nguyen, he co-wrote the Eisner-nominated *Batman: Li'l Gotham.* He's also worked on a range of titles including *Arkham City* with Paul Dini, *Adventures of Superman*, *Detective Comics*, *Sensation Comics Featuring Wonder Woman*, and *Biff to the Future* with producer/screenwriter Bob Gale. He's written and drawn comics based on the cartoons for *Adventure Time*, *Regular Show*, *Clarence*, *Pig Goat Banana Cricket*, *Pink Panther's The Inspector*, *Dexter's Laboratory*, *Teenage Mutant Ninja Turtles*, *Teen Titans Go!*, *Looney Tunes*, and *Scooby-Doo, Where Are You!* He's also written chapter books for Capstone based on the Justice League.

Dave Bardin

Dave Bardin is an award-winning illustrator who has worked in comics, commercials, music videos, video games, magazines, television, and book publishing. He has illustrated over twenty children's books including titles for Bad Robot, Graphic India, Leap Frog, Little Brown, Scholastic, Pearson, ABDO, Cartoon Network, Marvel, and DC. He lives and works in Los Angeles.